Hamfist Out
The Chill Is Gone

G. E. Nolly

Version 2014.01.03

ISBN 978-0-9754362-8-8

Special thanks to John Pratt and Gary Green for their outstanding editorial support.

Cover photo of author during pre-strike refueling, taken by Dr. Rob Naylor.

This book is dedicated to all military veterans, past, present and future.

Prologue

May 6, 1973

No matter how many times I had strapped on the F-4, entering it never got easier. The bird stood tall. The cockpit was eight feet above the tarmac, and climbing up the ladder with my helmet bag and my map case without busting my ass was difficult even in the daytime. During the pre-dawn darkness it was a real bitch.

At least I had a ladder. At Ubon, when we had a mass launch of airplanes during Operation Linebacker, we sometimes had to use the built-in drop-down steps that telescoped out of the fuselage. That was an accident waiting to happen.

I was already sweating profusely. There was no breeze at all, and my Nomex flight suit was clinging to me like it was made of Saran Wrap.

I craned my neck around to talk to Sergeant Adams, my Crew Chief, who was precariously perched on the edge of the cockpit, leaning over me and fastening my harness into the parachute quick release fasteners

"Looks like it's going to be a hot one again today,

Sarge."

"Yes, sir. Summer's bad enough at Kadena, but they say it's really going to be brutal here at CCK."

I turned again to answer him, but he was already at the rear cockpit helping my back-seater strap in.

I checked my Rolex and set the aircraft clock. As an FNG – Fucking New Guy – in the squadron, I didn't want to make a name for myself by being late at start-up and check-in. I was Number Two in this four-ship flight, and wanted to acquit myself well.

Captain John Clapp was Flight Lead. Naturally, his nickname was Drip. I hadn't ever flown on his wing before, and I didn't know him very well. He wasn't particularly friendly with any of us who had come to the squadron recently. I got the impression he had a hard-on for anyone with combat time, since he had spent his entire time flying F-4s in peacetime. Not my problem, his loss.

I breezed through the cockpit set-up, started the engines exactly on schedule, and listened up on Ground Control frequency.

"Tiger Flight, check."

"Two."

"Three."

Tiger Four didn't answer.

"Tiger Flight, listen up," Drip transmitted. "Tiger Four was an MND, so we'll be launching as a three-ship."

"Two copies."

"Three copies."

So, before we even got our engines started, we were one plane short. I had heard that Maintenance was really on its ass, and this Maintenance Non Delivery seemed to prove it. Coming from my previous environment, where we launched 64 airplanes at a time, and had ground running spares, this seemed incomprehensible to me.

Other than our local daytime training flights to the gunnery range, our wing only flew two four-ship missions a day, this Dawn Patrol and an evening Dusk Patrol. It sure didn't seem like it should be that difficult.

The Dawn and Dusk Patrols were important missions. We were helping the Taiwanese Air Force patrol the Straits of Taiwan, which were protected by friendly aircraft 24 hours every day. Every day, we flew an hour in the morning and an hour in the evening with our F-4Cs, and the Taiwanese pilots patrolled in their F-104s the rest of the day. All we had to do was provide two hours of coverage each day, and we were letting them down.

We taxied out to the quick-check area and received more bad news.

"Tiger Lead, this is Three."

"Go ahead, Three."

"The mechanic tells me he's found a hydraulic leak, and I'm a no-go."

"Are you safe to taxi?"

"Affirmative."

"Roger, you're cleared out of the formation, and you can return to the blocks."

Great. Now our morning four-ship has turned into a two-ship. It would be just our luck the great yellow horde picks this morning to invade.

After we left the quick-check area, we taxied to the arming area. The armament guys checked our munitions, and pulled our pins. Unlike my missions at Ubon, I didn't have any bombs. Strictly air-to-air munitions, radar-guided AIM-7 Sparrows and heat-seeking AIM-9E Sidewinders. And, unlike at Ubon, we'd be doing a formation takeoff. I hadn't performed a formation takeoff since F-4 RTU. This was going to be fun.

We took the runway together and held in position just as the sun rose over the horizon. At exactly our scheduled takeoff time, we received our takeoff clearance, and Drip tapped his helmet. Then he jerked his head forward and we lit our afterburners in perfect synchronization. Lead carried slightly less than full burner, to give me a little room with power to stay in formation in case my engine was producing slightly less thrust than his. Then it was liftoff, gear up on Drip's nod, flaps up the same way, and over to Departure Control.

"Tiger Flight, button two, go."

"Two."

Biff Birkman, my WSO, had our radio channelized on Channel Two in a heartbeat. It was nice having a good Weapon Systems Officer in the back seat. A weak WSO can make even the best pilot look bad, by not having the radios tuned quickly enough for check-in, or a hundred other things. Biff was making me look good. We went through the requisite frequencies as we headed west toward our patrol area, a north-south orbit about 60 miles in length, and checked in with the GCI site — Ground Control Intercept – that monitored the straits.

"Tiger check."

"Two."

"PyraMaid Control, Tiger flight of two fox fours, one hour playtime."

"Roger, Tiger Flight. Unknown rider at your one o'clock, thirty-three miles, heading east, angels unknown."

We were heading south. That meant the unidentified aircraft had originated from the west, in Mainland China. This was starting to get interesting.

I checked with my WSO on interphone. "Biff, are you painting him on your radar?"

"Negative, Hamfist, but I'm seeing an area that looks like chaff."

Distance to target was 24 miles now, and it was obvious the ingressing aircraft didn't want us to pick him up on radar. I'd used chaff many times, and it only had one purpose – to confuse enemy radar.

Back when I was flying up over Hanoi, during Operation Linebacker, and again during Linebacker II, it was routine for us to stuff chaff packets in the speed brakes. Each packet was a cardboard box about ten inches long, about five inches wide, and about an inch thick. It was crammed with thousands of thin strands of aluminum foil, looking just like the tinsel I used to put on our Christmas tree when I was a kid. When we were over the target area, if SAM sites were painting us, we would momentarily deploy our speed brakes and the chaff would fall out into the slipstream. At over 400 knots, the chaff packets would instantly rip open and saturate the air with tinsel. The SAM site's radar would be temporarily blind.

Whoever this was, he didn't want us to get a lock on him.

"Tiger Lead, this is Two. We're painting an area of chaff at one o'clock 22 miles."

"Roger, Two. Be advised my radar is bent."

Shit. Fucking Maintenance can only deliver two flyable airplanes out of four, and the radar doesn't work on one of them. Great, just fucking great. At least my radar was working. For now.

Lead wagged the tail of his aircraft, signaling for me to move from close-in "fingertip" position to "fighting wing" position. As we closed to about ten miles, we could see the sunlight glinting off an aircraft, down low, at about 500 feet altitude, headed east at a high rate of speed. We visually performed a left closing stern conversion, rolling out about three miles in trail. As we were abeam the aircraft during the conversion, we got a positive ID on him. It was a Badger. To be more accurate, it was a Xian H-6, a Chinese variation of the Russian TU-16 Badger bomber.

Because we had been up-sun from the H-6, he probably hadn't seen us.

"Tiger Flight, arm 'em up."

"Two."

Our Rules of Engagement were very specific. With the Straits of Taiwan only a little over 100 miles wide, there was no room for error. We were to fire on any aircraft headed from China to Taiwan. There simply wouldn't be time to go through any involved clearance process. Bad guy comes in, we shoot him down. It was as simple as that.

We were now only about a mile in trail with the bomber. I had been expecting Drip to pass the flight lead over to me, since my radar was still operational and his wasn't. That meant he couldn't fire his AIM-7 and I could still try to fire mine. But he didn't pass the lead to me. That meant he was going to close in for a Fox-2 attack, using his AIM-9E heat-seeking missiles. I instantly knew Drip had shitty flight discipline.

I thought back of the story that Colonel West, our DO at Homestead, had told us, when I was going through F-4 training.

"During Operation Rolling Thunder, an F-105 flight lead was in an extended engagement with a MiG. He was performing repeated high-speed yoyos, gaining on the MiG with each yoyo. One more yoyo and he would be in a firing position."

The Colonel paused and looked around the room. We were all transfixed in rapt attention.

"Just as he was about to get a firing solution, his wingman called Bingo."

Bingo meant that the fuel had reached the predetermined quantity where the flight must Return To Base.

"What do you think Lead did?"

Colonel West made eye contact with each of us. I was hoping he wasn't expecting any of us to answer.

"Lead did what he was supposed to do," he continued, "he disengaged by doing a quarter roll and zoom, and he RTB'd. And I'll tell you why he did it. He did it because he had flight discipline. And he had trust. He trusted that his wingman wouldn't call Bingo unless he was really at Bingo fuel. And he, the Flight Lead, had established that Bingo. He gave up his MiG because he had discipline. If he had taken one more slice, done one more yoyo, he could have had that MiG. But he would have put his wingman in jeopardy. He did the right thing. He had discipline."

If Drip had passed the lead to me, I could have performed a Fox-1 attack with my Sparrows, and had a better chance of scoring a kill from a distance. Then I could have followed up with an AIM-9E attack if needed. Now we were too close to engage with the AIM-7s. More important, the AIM-9E only had a 20-pound warhead, one fourth the size of the warhead on the AIM-7.

The aural tone of my Sidewinder was growling in my headset. That meant it was seeing a heat signature.

My missile was ready to go, like a race horse straining at the bit.

Then, finally, Drip did what he had to do. He passed me the lead.

"Tiger Two, Lead. I have no tone." He sounded totally spent. "You have the lead. Cleared to fire."

Maintenance had scored a perfect trifecta: broken airplanes, broken radar, broken missiles.

I took the lead position, put the H-6 in my gun site, waited for a solid tone, and fired my first Sidewinder.

1

April 9, 1973

Ching Chuan Kang Air Base – CCK – in central Taiwan was the last thing I had anticipated when I received my assignment to Kadena Air Base, in Okinawa. When I signed in at the squadron at Kadena, I had expected the typical bustle of people milling around the squadron, plus crews in the briefing rooms and the usual flurry of activity. Instead, I walked into an empty building.

Not totally empty. There was one person, Staff Sergeant Molloy, standing behind the Duty Desk.

"Good morning, sir. Would you be Captain Hancock?"

"That would be me. What happened to everyone?"

"The squadron is on permanent TDY to CCK, sir. You have up to ten days to in-process on base here at Kadena, then you'll be deploying to CCK."

"What do you mean by permanent TDY?"

"Well, sir, anyone who goes TDY for more than 179 days gets credit for a remote tour, and gets sent back to the States. So our guys go over for 175 days or so, then they come back here to Kadena to tag up at home plate before they go back to CCK. They usually ferry an airplane back here for maintenance that can't be performed at CCK."

"How long do they get to stay here at Kadena?"

"Usually two or three days," he answered. "Depends on the needs of the service and how fast the airplanes get fixed."

"How long has that been going on?"

"Commando Domino started last November."

I had heard the term Commando Domino as the war in Vietnam was winding down, but didn't realize it involved sending guys TDY for extended periods. I had thought it was just a transfer of airplanes.

"Tell me about this Domino operation."

"Well, sir, just before we signed a peace accord with North Vietnam, we pumped up the South Vietnamese military with a ton of equipment. We didn't have a lot of airplanes to give to them, so we talked the Chinese – that would be the good guy Chinese in Taiwan — into transferring their F-5s to South Vietnam, and we would give them brand-new F-5Es. In the meantime, until they get their new airplanes, we'll help them with their air defense."

"So," I asked, "the F-4s from the 18th Tactical Fighter Wing are in CCK to help with the air defense of Taiwan?"

"That's about it, sir. We're going to be doing it until they get their new F-5s. Probably about a year."

This was the second time in my short Air Force career I was hit with a bolt totally out of the blue. When I had gotten assigned to Yokota Air Base, outside Tokyo, to fly T-39's in 1970, I hadn't expected to be going TDY for three months at a time. Now, just when I thought I'd be in a regular peacetime fighter squadron, I find out I'll be on extended TDY. It would probably be just my luck I'd be gone when our baby was born in the summer.

"Where do I go to process in?"

"Here's your in-processing package, sir," he replied, handing me a thick, large envelope, "all the forms you need are in there, and I've also included a map of the base so you can find everything. Start here, at CBPO," he pointed to a location on the map, "and they will direct you to the other base facilities."

"Okay, thanks, Sarge."

"And sir," he said, as I was leaving, "Welcome to Kadena."

I had flown through Kadena Air Base often when I had been operating T-39s out of Yokota, and had spent the night on numerous occasions, so I pretty much knew my way around base. There was a shuttle bus that provided regular service around the base, and I used the shuttle to get to the Consolidated Base Personnel Office to start my in-processing.

In addition to the routine forms to complete at CBPO, I had to process through the Finance Office. One of the really neat programs they had was the ability to take an advance of three month's salary with every PCS – Permanent Change of Station – assignment. It basically boiled down to an interest-free loan, to be paid back by payroll deductions over the course of the next year. It was a way for servicemen to get money for furnishing quarters and other expenses incidental to a PCS move. I took advantage of the program, and promptly deposited it into an account I had opened at the bank on base. With a baby on the way, I was pretty sure we'd find good use for the money.

There were a lot of other places I had to go, like the Flight Records section, the Base Dental Facility, the Flight Surgeon's office and the Education Office. With numerous waits for the shuttle bus, it was slow going. I spent the better part of three days conducting my in-processing activities. The biggest surprise was the housing situation at Kadena.

It was grim.

2

April 9, 1973

I had to get a phone call through to Samantha. Her joint spouse assignment to Kadena was scheduled to begin in May, and I wanted to see if she could get it delayed, at least until we could arrange for base housing.

It turned out housing on base was at a real premium. It wasn't unusual for families to have to wait more than a year to get billeted on base. That meant they'd have to rent apartments or houses in the village outside the base. Not the best environment. Or, they could get on-base housing at Naha Air Base, at the southern tip of the island, right away. The problem with that solution was that the drive from Naha to Kadena could take over an hour during morning rush hour traffic. And once anyone was assigned housing at Naha, he couldn't transfer to Kadena housing. He'd be locked in at Naha for his entire three-and-a-half year tour of duty.

I didn't want Sam having to deal with that all by herself, especially in her delicate condition. She had already shown numerous times how strong and resourceful she was, but I would be constantly worried about her. So, for my sake more than hers, I wanted her to delay her assignment.

When I had been flying T-39s out of Yokota, I usually stopped in at the MAC Command Post every time I transited Kadena. I had gotten to know most of the officers working there pretty well, so I decided to pay a visit to see if any of the guys I knew were still there. I went up to the fortified door, stood in front of the one-way mirrored window, and pressed the buzzer. After a few seconds, the door opened. Major Don Watson burst through the doorway.

"Ham! How the hell are you doing? I've heard nothing but great things about you! I told everybody if they wanted to get the war over and done with, they needed to send you!"

"Well," I grinned, "I had a little help, but I did most of it by myself."

He gave me a bear hug like I was his long-lost brother, then he held me at arm's length to look me over.

"You look like you lost weight."

"You should have seen me three weeks ago, before I got some of Sam's cooking."

Don motioned for me to enter the dimly-lit

Command Post. Don had met Sam three years earlier, when we'd had a military RON – Remain Over Night – when our T-39 mission to Hong Kong had spent the night at Kadena because of a maintenance issue with the airplane. Sam had been on official TDY orders to attend a legal conference in Hong Kong, and was on the mission with me.

Don had been immediately captivated by Sam, like everyone else who'd met her. He'd insisted on taking us out to dinner at his favorite restaurant off-base, a place called Sam's By The Sea. The place was decorated with numerous photos of the actors from the movie *Teahouse of the August Moon*, which had been filmed there. We'd had a delicious seafood dinner, and had become close friends with Don.

"How's that smoking hot wife of yours doing? When am I going to see her again?"

"We got a joint spouse assignment here, so you may see her sooner than you think. And speaking of cooking, she's got a bun in the oven."

"Fantastic! When's she due?"

"Beginning of July. I just hope I can be with her when she delivers. I may be TDY."

"So, you're in the 18th."

I nodded.

Don looked down at the floor. "Those guys are being run ragged. Permanent TDY. Total bullshit. It's tearing families apart, with no end in sight."

"We get calls from wives here," he continued. "They think we're the Wing Command Post. They don't understand that we're Military Airlift Command, not part of your wing. Anyway, you wouldn't believe the things that are happening to the families here. Kids using drugs. Teenagers streaking. Some wives making suicide attempts. Really sad."

I wanted to change the subject.

"Don, any chance I could use the autovon?"

The autovon was the military telephone system for long-distance calls.

"Only if you're going to call your bride. Here," he motioned to a sound-proofed room, "this is the room we use for secure calls. You can talk as long as you want, and you'll have all the privacy you need."

My eyes were beginning to adjust to the dim illumination, and I could see three enlisted men at their consoles on the opposite side of the room. Don turned to them.

"Gentlemen, this is Captain Hamilton Hancock. He's the most genuine war hero you'll ever meet, and he gets priority for autovon calls any time he wants. Any questions?"

They answered pretty much in unison, "No sir."

I entered the room and shut the door behind me. It closed with a muffled thud.

I wasn't looking forward to this conversation.

3

April 17, 1973

I arrived at CCK early in the morning after a late-night flight on a C-130. I followed Sergeant Molloy's directions and found the squadron building with no problem. There was a temporary sign in front of the building that announced our squadron's presence. Because we were a TDY squadron, and simply tenants on this C-130 base, none of the buildings of the 18th Tactical Fighter Wing had permanent signs.

When I entered the squadron, I was back in familiar territory. There were lots of guys in flight suits, and everyone wanted to introduce himself and welcome me. After a few minutes, a portly Lieutenant Colonel emerged from the Operations Officer's office.

"You must be Captain Hancock," he said, holding out his hand, "Welcome to CCK. I'm Bob Milner."

"Pleased to meet you, sir. I'm glad to be here."

"Why don't you come into my office, and we'll have a little chat."

I followed him into his office and we sat next to each other in the soft leather chairs that were set apart from his desk.

"I think you're really going to like your assignment here," he began, "we have a great mix of DOCs."

"Excuse me, sire, what's a DOC?"

"Designed Operational Capability. Some wings only have air-to-air DOC, some have air-to-ground. We have air-to-air, air-to-ground, and nuclear, so you'll be getting a terrific variety of mission profiles."

"We use our air-to-air DOC every day when we fly our Dawn Patrol and Dusk Patrol missions."

"What are the Dawn Patrol and Dusk Patrol?" I asked. I had heard a little about them, but wasn't sure exactly what they were.

"The Straits of Taiwan are patrolled 24 hours every day to guard against an air invasion by the Communist Chinese. The Taiwanese Air Force uses F-104 aircraft and flies twenty-two four-ship missions a day. We fly two four-ship 1-hour missions every day, one early in the morning, the Dawn Patrol, and one in the evening, the Dusk Patrol."

"As the war in Vietnam was winding down," he continued. "the Russians and Chinese were pumping up the North Vietnamese military with tanks, airplanes, everything. We, the United States, were doing the same thing with the South Vietnamese. But we didn't have enough airplanes to give them, so we asked the Taiwanese to provide their F-5s to South Vietnam. They were using their F-5s for air defense, so the United States offered to loan two squadrons of F-4s to help out with their air defense until they receive replacement airplanes, new F-5Es. That's why the 18th Tactical Fighter Wing is over here."

It sounded interesting. "You said we also do air-to-ground and nuclear?"

"Yes. We use the Ie Shima bombing range, back in Okinawa, for our delivery practice. The air-to-ground is standard conventional deliveries, and the nuclear is low-level loft deliveries. Plus, of course, a lot of training in everything that goes along with the nuclear DOC. No-lone-zone procedures, PAL enabling, launch codes, lots of fun stuff," he said, with a wry smile.

I got the distinct impression the nuclear training was not going to be so much fun.

"We have you set up to start Indoc Training tomorrow, and we hope to have you Combat Ready in about two months."

"Sir, I just came from combat. Why would it take me two months to get Combat Ready?"

He stiffened. "This is not Southeast Asia, where training and documentation took a back seat to everything else. Our unit has a C-status to maintain.

Right now we're C-1, and we plan to stay that way. Every crewmember has to be trained and take a check ride in each DOC to be designated Combat Ready. If we don't have enough crews Combat Ready, we will lose our C-1 status, degrade to C-2 or even C-3. You have a lot of training ahead of you, Captain."

I thought back to when I was at Ubon. We'd had a large, athletic Lieutenant Colonel, John Wilkie, in the squadron. He'd been flying fighters his entire career. He'd flown in F-86s in Korea as a Lieutenant, and had flown a plethora of other fighters, with tons of time in the F-100, with overseas assignments to France and Libya. We called him Big John.

"War is hell," Big John used to say, "but peace is a real bitch."

I was starting to understand what Big John was alluding to.

"Let's talk about additional duties," Lieutenant Colonel Milner said, "we have several openings." He retrieved a sheet of paper from his desk and handed it to me. "Are you interested in any of these?"

Additional duties were required of every crewmember, and ran the gamut from Admin Officer to Snack Bar Officer and everything in between. While most of us wanted to simply fly, we all knew that the things we would learn from performing our additional duties would give us experience in non-flying activities, experience we would need if and when we assumed more senior positions, such as Flight Commanders, Operations Officers, Squadron Commanders and, perhaps, even more. Also, the additional duties provided fodder for the narratives on our Officer Effectiveness Reports. OERs were the "report cards" used by promotion boards to determine who would advance to higher rank.

I looked over the sheet.

"Well, sir, I was Life Support Officer at my squadron at Ubon. In fact, I completed the ECI Life Support Officer Course and received an additional AFSC for Life Support Officer. I enjoyed it, and wouldn't mind doing it again. But I'm more than happy to take any of these other jobs also."

When I was at Ubon, I had learned that the year transpired a lot quicker if there was something to do when we weren't flying. ECI courses were a great way to pass the time and enhance a professional resume. The ECI courses were home-study courses provided by the Air Force's Extension Course Institute. They were fairly comprehensive, and successful completion would earn the participant an additional Air Force Specialty Code – AFSC – that signified expertise in that area. It was like a grown-up merit badge that provided entry into an additional career field.

"Okay," he said, drawing a line through Life

Support Officer on his sheet, "you're our new Life Support Officer."

"One more thing, Captain Hancock," the Lieutenant Colonel Milner said, as he rose and walked me toward his office door, "you'll need to remove that Hundred Mission patch from your flight suit. The only patches authorized by Air Force Regulation 35-10 are the squadron patch, the Tactical Air Command Patch and the Pacific Air Forces patch. Save your other patches for your party suit."

The party suit was a short-sleeve flight suit, usually in some color other than green, that we would wear to casual squadron get-togethers. There were always tailor shops around every base that could make party suits in one or two days. Typical party suit colors were red or yellow, and most party suits had numerous patches from prior units. Some guys' party suits had so many patches they looked like helmet bags.

"Yes, sir," I said, as I saluted and left his office.

Yeah, peace was going to be a real bitch.

4

April 17, 1973

I was a assigned a BOQ – Bachelor Officer Quarters – room with another Captain, Duke Donaldson. I knew Duke from our time together at Ubon. He had been in a different squadron, but I had flown on his wing a few times when I first arrived at Ubon, when they were intermixing squadron missions. His previous tour had been in F-105s – Thuds – and he was one of the first guys at Ubon to qualify for a 100-mission patch.

"Nice to see you again, Hamfist" he said, as he gestured toward the empty bed and desk that would be mine, "You won't *believe* the bullshit level of the peacetime Air Force!"

"I'd heard about it, but this was my first taste of it. Colonel Milner said it would take me two months to get Combat Ready."

"Yeah. That's about what it took for me. Two months! And did Milner give you a ration of shit about your patch?" he asked, pointing to my Hundred Mission patch.

"Yep. He quoted 35-10 to me."

"35-10 is a big deal here," Duke said, "Haircuts, sleeves on flight suits not rolled up, and making sure mustaches don't extend beyond, get this, *the vermilion of the lips*. And no crush in the flight cap."

"Wow!"

"Welcome to the peace-time Air Force."

"Is it like this everywhere?" I asked.

"Pretty much so, from what I hear. But, at least here, once you get past the bullshit, the flying is really great. The Taiwanese love us. We can fly pretty much anywhere we want, and as low as we want. Their attitude about us is that the roar of our engines is the sound of freedom."

"I'm really looking forward to getting back into the air."

"Have you met Cocktail yet?" Duke asked.

"Who's Cocktail?"

"Cocktail Collins, our Squadron Commander.

"I didn't see him at the squadron when I was there."

"It doesn't surprise me you haven't met him yet. He's not around a whole lot. When he's not flying, he's either drinking or sleeping. He didn't get that nickname by accident."

"But I'll tell you something," he continued, "he's the best fighter pilot in the squadron. Usually his hand is shaking so much he can hardly get his cigarette to his mouth in the preflight briefing, but he wins the money every time we go to the range. Every time. Best bombs I've ever seen."

5

April 21, 1973

I had spent the previous four days at Indoctrination Training. Indoc was a fairly formal class, run by the Wing Weapons Officer, Bo Bosworth. Bo was a very sharp Captain, a graduate of the USAF Fighter Weapons School. He took what could have been a dry subject and made it interesting.

First, we learned about the local flying environment. CCK Air Base was located next to the town of Taichung, near the center of the island of Taiwan. The north-south runway at CCK was located just a few miles north-northwest of the short north-south runway of Taichung Airport. This was a set-up for some unsuspecting pilot to land at the wrong airport during an approach in limited visibility. I was really glad Bo told me about it before I embarrassed myself.

There was an emergency landing facility at Tainan, at the south end of the island, and an additional base at Ping Tung, not far from Tainan. To the north, Taipei International Airport could also be used if the single runway at CCK became disabled.

Although there was a bombing range in Taiwan,

our primary bombing range was on Ie Shima Island, in Okinawa. This necessitated fairly long, four-hour missions to conduct our air-to-ground training. Naturally, in the event of any problems, our primary emergency airport during air-to-ground training would be Kadena Air Base.

We learned a lot more about the Dawn Patrol and Dusk Patrol missions. Our tasking was managed by the Air Division, which was located in Taipei. The Air Division would be calling the shots for our air defense mission.

Overall, I felt Indoc training was excellent, and I was ready to start flying.

Every afternoon the crews of both fighter squadrons would assemble at the bar in the CCK Officers Club. The O'Club was an excellent facility. In addition to the bar, they had a terrific restaurant. And the prices were really great. I really enjoyed the camaraderie of a bunch of fighter jocks standing around, swapping stories and getting to know each other. It didn't take long for me to get to know everyone in the squadron.

We wore our flight suits in the bar, because we were normally there fairly early in the day. Because we were a tenant unit on base, the C-130 wing established the rules, and the edict for the bar was that no flight suits were allowed after 1900 hours – seven in the evening. That usually wasn't a problem, since we typically were finished drinking before that. And a lot of the time, the guys would wear civvies to the bar, because they would either go to the restaurant afterward or proceed to downtown Taichung. And we always wore civvies off base.

There was a commercial bus that stopped at several places on base, then proceeded to take the occupants into Taichung. The bus was called the Smoker, and the last stop before heading downtown was in front of the Officer's Club. Duke had introduced me to the Smoker and had shown me around Taichung a few days earlier, and I enjoyed walking around the city, taking in the sights and shopping for souvenirs. There were a bunch of nice jewelry stores in town, and I was hoping Sam would get a chance to visit CCK soon, so I could show her around. Maybe buy her something nice.

There was another side of Taichung that some of the guys visited. The area was called the Dirty Dozen, twelve bars that were actually whorehouses. Every bar reportedly had gorgeous girls, and the most beautiful, and most famous, was a madam named Cee-Cee. She had become a legend in her own time, and had established a reputation that had spread throughout the Air Force.

Automatic Terminal Information Service, called ATIS, was a service that was provided to pilots at every

Air Force base. Basically, as you were preparing to takeoff or land, you would tune in the ATIS on a special radio frequency and hear a pre-recorded message that would provide airfield information, such as wind direction, altimeter setting, temperature and runway in use. The recording would change about every hour, or whenever the weather or runway condition changed. Using ATIS eliminated the previous requirement to call the tower on the radio to find out the weather and runway. Pilots still called the tower for takeoff and landing clearance, but only after learning the routine non-control information.

There was a story, maybe bullshit, maybe not, that one day the CCK ATIS recording contained the phrase, "Attention all aircrews: Charlie Charlie has Victor Delta." Charlie is the phonetic alphabet letter C, Victor is the phonetic alphabet letter V, and Delta is the phonetic alphabet letter D. In other words, "Cee-Cee has VD".

On this day I was at the bar at about 1730 hours, having a quick drink – just a Coke – before heading back to the BOQ to study. I had just enrolled in the Air Command And Staff College course through ECI, and wanted to get a running start. ACSC was part of the Professional Military Education – PME – required for promotion to Major. I had already completed the previous prerequisite PME course, Squadron Officer School, while I was at Ubon.

Lieutenant Colonel Milner approached me with a

drink in his hand. He seemed a bit unsteady on his feet, and he smelled of gin as he leaned toward me.

"The Smoker is leaving for downtown in twenty-five minutes," he slurred, "Mandatory formation. We're going to introduce you to the Dirty Dozen and get your horns trimmed. I'll get Cee-Cee to show you her tits."

"Thank you, sir," I replied, "but I have a date with some PME, so I'll pass."

This wasn't my first rodeo when it came to guys trying to get me to go whoring with them. At Ubon, there was normally a standard group of guys who would go to the massage parlors en masse pretty much every night for the famous Rub and Scrub, a great massage with a "happy ending" at one of the numerous massage parlors near the base. The Thai girls who worked at the parlors were beautiful, and a lot of the guys referred to them as LBFMs – Little Brown Fucking Machines. I'd had a Rub and Scrub the first time I went to NKP Air Base, in Thailand, after making an emergency landing in Laos, and it was a memorable experience.

But that was back before I was married. I was a married man when I was stationed at Ubon, and I left the massage parlor scene to the bachelors and the guys who called themselves "Class-B bachelors". Every now and then one of the guys would try to get me to go to a Rub and Scrub with the group, and I'd just say I wasn't interested. No harm, no foul. I'd been faithful to Sam ever since meeting her, and I planned to stay that way.

"Maybe you didn't hear what I said, Captain," Milner said, swaying as he poked his finger into my chest, "It's a mandatory formation. You better be on that bus."

He turned and staggered away before I could respond. I finished my Coke and returned to my room. Naturally, I didn't go downtown with Milner and the gang. I harbored the hope that he was so drunk he wouldn't remember our encounter.

No such luck.

6

April 22, 1973

It's no fun being on the Ops Officer's shit list. There are an unlimited number of ways the Ops Officer can make life miserable for a pilot, some obvious, some not so much.

I showed up at the squadron to fly a morning training mission. When I looked at the lineup on the large plastic board behind the duty desk that showed the day's flying schedule, I saw my name crossed off in red grease pencil. I looked at the board to see if I had been reassigned to a different mission. I had. I was going to spend the day as RSO.

The Runway Supervisory Officer was the person who manned the Runway Supervisory Unit, a small trailer located alongside the runway at the approach end. It looked like the cab of a typical control tower, and was equipped with a console with radios that could be used to communicate with aircraft on tower frequency. The RSU also had a guarded switch that could be used to fire remote-control flares, to warn airplanes that they were not permitted to land. If the RSO saw an aircraft approaching without the landing gear extended, he was expected to call the aircraft on the radio, and follow up by firing a flare.

RSO was really a job suited for an enlisted troop. I'd heard that the Marines would use an enlisted man to perform RSU duty. They would promise him a case of beer for every gear-up landing he prevented.

Having an RSO look over landing aircraft seemed like the pilots were being treated like children. It cost a minimum of one million dollars to train the pilot of an F-4. The pilots are mature, professional aviators. The checklist used for landing required that the pilot confirm landing gear extension. In addition, there was another crewmember in each F-4. It was extremely unlikely that an aircraft would land gear up. And the tower controllers visually checked each landing aircraft to ensure that the gear was down. But still, there were RSUs, and they needed to be manned.

Usually, the new Lieutenants on their first flying assignment performed RSO duty. It was a way of paying their dues.

And now, as a Captain with three flying assignments under my belt, two in combat, I was assigned RSO duty. It seemed pretty clear to me I was on the Ops Officer's shit list, and I figured it couldn't get much worse.

In about a month I would learn just how much worse it could get.

7

May 6, 1973

My AIM-9 hit the H-6 directly in his number one engine, and his left wing completely separated from the aircraft. I saw two crewmembers eject upward, and, about one second later, two crewmembers ejected downward as the aircraft started wildly tumbling. I saw no other survivors. As flight lead, at least temporarily, it was my responsibility to notify Taiwanese authorities.

"PyraMaid, Tiger flight has an enemy aircraft down and four survivors in the water at our present position."

"Roger, Tiger flight. We'll notify rescue."

Just as I was about to respond, a missile, much larger than an AIM-9, went past my aircraft in the direction of my travel, directly below my right wing. I initially thought one of my AIM-7s had fired. Biff was now screaming in my headset, and I couldn't tell if he was on hot mike or transmitting on UHF.

"We have a MiG at six o'clock!"

I looked in my mirror and saw a camouflaged MiG-19 behind and above me. It was the first time I had ever seen a blue and grey camouflage scheme. I got on the radio.

"Tiger flight, BREAK!"

Drip was on my left wing and broke hard left as I broke hard right. If we were lucky, the MiG would follow Drip, and I would be able to get on his tail and hose him with one of my missiles. If we weren't lucky, he would follow me. Since Drip didn't have any operational missiles, he couldn't do our flight any good.

We weren't lucky. The MiG was on my tail.

I immediately started a scissors maneuver to see what the MiG pilot was made of.

And I thought about the OODA loop.

8

May 6, 1973

Instantly, I remembered a conversation I'd had over breakfast at the Ubon Officers Club.

When I was at Ubon, a year earlier, I had heard about the OODA loop from Springs Springer, the squadron Weapons Officer, one of the most experienced F-4 jocks in the squadron. Springs had attended the USAF Fighter Weapons School at Nellis Air Force Base, in Las Vegas, and had been the Distinguished Graduate in his class. Fighter Weapons School is the PhD of fighter flying. Springs really knew his stuff.

"Springs," I asked, "what's the most important thing to do to win an engagement?"

Springs looked down at his plate and picked at his omelet.

"Eat a good breakfast."

"What?" I was shocked. I thought he was going to tell me to keep the burner lit, perform some fancy maneuver that I would have trouble visualizing, or try a low-speed scissors.

"When I was at Nellis, I learned about the OODA loop, and I learned that the guy who has the fighter pilot's breakfast is the guy who loses the fight."

The mythical "fighter pilot's breakfast" was purported to be a coke, a cigarette and a barf.

"You win the fight," he continued, *"by getting a good night's sleep and having a good breakfast. That way, your brain is functioning at peak performance. You need your brain operating at its max capacity to Observe, Orient, Decide and Act. OODA. OODA was developed by John Boyd, a really great fighter pilot. John was known as '40-second Boyd', because he claimed he could win any engagement within 40 seconds, starting with his opponent behind him. He had a standing bet. And he never lost. He did it using his brain."*

"Did you ever fight him?" I asked.

"Yes. Once."

"And...?"

"I thought I told you. He never lost a bet."

I was grateful I'd had a good breakfast before this Dawn Patrol. Ever since my conversation with Springs, I'd made a concerted effort to get a good night's sleep and eat a good breakfast. Sometimes the two were mutually exclusive, since I would need to get up about an hour earlier to get to the O'Club and eat without being rushed. But I always ate breakfast. Every day.

I lit the burner to pick up some smash and started a scissors maneuver, quickly rolling right, then left, then again reversing direction. After about six cycles, I performed a high-AOA vector roll, looking in my mirrors and over my shoulder to see the MiG pilot's reaction. If he was unskilled, he would have been flushed out in front of me. *Observe*.

This MiG pilot was no beginner. He counter-rolled and stayed behind me. I unloaded to zero G's and continued my scissors. I didn't want him to get a tracking solution on me.

Use your brain, Hamfist, use your brain. *Orient*.

I discontinued the scissors and pulled up to vertical, using max burner. I knew he'd follow me. As soon as I was vertical, I started another scissors, this time going straight up. *Decide*.

I could see the MiG was not falling behind. If he had been falling behind, it would have meant his energy level was below mine, and I would have continued going straight up until he fell off. Then I would do a quick reversal and be on his tail headed downhill.

He was staying with me, headed uphill. *Act*.

I had studied the Vertical Rolling Scissors maneuver

in RTU, but had never performed it in flight. Our instructor in class had been using his hands, "shooting down his watch", trying to explain how the maneuver worked. We never got to try it in training, but I thought I had a good grasp of the concept. It was time to see if I could do it. I performed a vector roll in the vertical.

The MiG was out in front of me like he was shot out of a gun. Now I was on his tail, but he didn't look flummoxed. He immediately pushed forward, performing a negative-G maneuver to head downhill. I rolled inverted and followed him down. He was outracing me, which was exactly what I wanted. I needed separation, for him to get within range for my AIM-9, and right now I was too close on his tail for my missiles to arm.

Finally, after what seemed like a lifetime, we had sufficient separation, and I had a solid tone in my headset. I rechecked my switches and fired my second sidewinder. The missile guided perfectly and went directly into his tail. The MiG exploded in a giant fireball.

I didn't see any ejection.

9

May 6, 1973

After the MiG-kill, Drip joined up on my left wing and transmitted, "Okay, Number Two, I have the lead."

"Roger, you have the lead." I put the light on the star, assuming standard fingertip position.

That was it. I was back to being a wingman as we returned to CCK. Other than the standard frequency changes, we flew back in radio silence.

When we checked in on CCK Tower frequency, the American controller transmitted, "Tiger Flight, you are cleared for a high-speed pass and closed pattern."

Apparently word of my in-flight victories had somehow filtered back to the base. During the war, when airplanes returned to their bases after scoring aerial kills, either in South Vietnam or in Thailand, they would perform a high-speed pass and then pull up sharply into a closed traffic pattern. Sometimes even an aileron roll on initial.

Drip wasn't interested in any of that. We flew a normal traffic pattern, a standard initial, followed by a five-second pitch-out to downwind, and in-trail landings. As we taxied toward the parking area, I saw a gathering of pilots standing around waiting for us. A couple guys were holding champagne bottles, and I saw one pilot with a can of spray paint and a stencil of a star. This was going to be really cool. It was obvious that it was my plane that had scored the victories, since Drip's plane still had all its missiles.

Just as we approached the parking spot, I saw a Colonel walk up to the group of pilots and talk to them, and they rapidly dispersed. The Colonel was waiting for me when I shut down the engines. I hadn't met this Colonel before, but I recognized him from his photo. He was Colonel Myers, the Acting Wing Commander for our detachment at CCK. The actual Wing Commander, a Brigadier General, was back at Kadena.

Sergeant Adams had a ladder up to the left side of the airplane as soon as my engines were shut down, and was instantly putting the pins in my ejection seat.

"I'm not sure what's going on, Captain, but I want to be the first to congratulate you."

"Thanks, Sarge. Any idea why the guys left the area?"

"Not really, sir. They were all gathering here to welcome you, and then Colonel Myers told them they had to leave. No idea why."

I descended the ladder and saluted the Colonel.

"Captain Hancock," he said sternly, "I know you believe that you scored an aerial victory…"

"Actually, sir," I interrupted, "it's two aerial victories." I hadn't intended to be rude, it just slipped out.

"I know you believe you scored two victories, but it never happened."

"Sir, I don't understand."

His face softened. "I'm really sorry, Hamilton, but we simply cannot acknowledge what happened today. The Chinese have been itching to start an international incident, and we just can't give them what they want. So this never happened. No celebrations, no victory laps, nothing special. I'm sorry. I really am."

"Yes, sir. I understand."

I saluted, he returned my salute, and I walked to the Life Support section to leave off my helmet and parachute harness.

So that was that. When I got to the squadron, a couple of the guys winked at me, but they were following orders by not talking about it. As far as we were all concerned, it never happened.

But I knew better, and that was all that really mattered to me. I didn't need any PDA – Public Display of Affection – I had the satisfaction of knowing I had entered a life-and-death duel with a highly skilled enemy pilot, and I had prevailed. They couldn't take that away from me.

10

May 8, 1973

Our squadron had been planning a joint dinner with the Taiwanese F-104 pilots for a few weeks. Our get-together had nothing to do with the activities from two days earlier, but the mood seemed decidedly more jovial than at our previous get-togethers.

In a completely unexpected move, the Taiwanese pilots had a rather formal ceremony and presented each of us with Taiwanese Air Force pilot wings. Because of Air Force regulations, we wouldn't be authorized to wear them on our uniforms, but it was still a really nice touch.

For dinner, we were seated around large round tables with about ten of us at each table. A lazy susan adorned the center of every table, and the waiters brought one course of food after another, with each of us taking a small amount from the center with the serving chopsticks and putting it on our dishes. There must have been close to twenty courses.

Then it was time for toasts. I was sitting next to a Taiwanese Air Force Captain. He turned to me, raised his wine glass, and said, "Here's to your mother. *Gom-*

bay." *Gom-bay* was the Chinese equivalent to "bottoms up".

I raised my glass, responded, "*Gom-bay,*" and downed my drink.

The Captain was looking at me expectantly. Then I caught on. I took the wine bottle from the table, filled his glass, then mine, and raised my glass.

"Here's to your mother. *Gom-bay.*"

Everyone at the table responded, "*Gom-bay.*"

We went around the table, making toasts. It turned out – big surprise – that everyone at the table had a mother and father. That came out to twenty drinks, not counting the sips of wine that had preceded the toasts. Naturally, I got shit-faced drunk.

The last thing I remember, I was leaving the dinner table with my arm around the shoulder of the Taiwanese Captain, yelling, "Just you and me against the field-graders."

I woke up some time that night, on my bed in the BOQ. The light was on, the door was open, and I had no recollection of how I got there. I was fully dressed, lying on top of the sheets. There was vomit all over the front of my clothing.

I think it was mine.

11

May 12, 1973

Only two bad things can happen to a fighter pilot: he goes out to his airplane knowing he is taking his last flight in a fighter, or he goes out to his airplane not knowing he is taking his last flight in a fighter.

I had been working pretty hard at my additional duty, trying to get the shop up to speed. The previous Life Support Officer had DEROSed almost six months earlier, and the shop had been running pretty much on autopilot. And there were a lot of things falling through the cracks.

There were overdue inspections on helmets and oxygen masks. Harnesses weren't being sent back to the parachute shop at the required inspection cycles. Crews weren't receiving their annual instruction on how to don and remove the "poopy suits" we had to wear when we flew over water. The list went on endlessly. I was putting in a lot of time at the Life Support section.

I was also spending a lot of my free time in the evenings trying to finish the first of the three volumes that made up the Air Command and Staff College course. There would be a written exam, administered by the Education Office, at the end of each section, and there was a lot to learn. So, even though I wasn't flying all that much, I still wasn't finding time to get a lot of sleep.

And I felt like shit. I had a constant low-grade fever and a headache that wasn't bad enough to see the Flight Surgeon about, but it was sure distracting. And the glands under my chin were constantly swollen and tender. I knew I needed to get more rest, but it seemed there just wasn't time.

Sam was going to be arriving on base in two more days. She'd arranged for seven days of leave, and I'd made a reservation at the Grand Hotel in downtown Taichung. When I went there to check the hotel out the week prior, I was impressed with how clean and modern the place was. I was really looking forward to having some quality time with Sam. I'd gotten the Life Support shop up to speed enough that it could coast for a week without my constant supervision, and I was pretty well ahead on my ECI course. So all I had to do for the next week was fly and spend my free time with Sam.

On this day, I had a ride to the gunnery range at Ie Shima. It was a fairly long mission, just over four hours, and I brought two canteens of water and three piddle packs with me in my helmet bag. As large and roomy as the F-4 cockpit appeared, there weren't a lot of places to put extra gear, since the entire cockpit consisted of switches, controls and indicators to operate every piece of equipment the airplane carried. When I was at Ubon I had discovered that I could secure the canteens and piddle packs, along with my helmet bag, on the left rear side of the cockpit, just next to the G-suit connector, and it would be out of the way.

I was incredibly thirsty the whole flight. I had finished off one canteen before we even got to the range. We were dropping BDU-33 practice bombs, and most of our deliveries were 45-degree dive. The bombs were released at 450 knots, and then we would need a 4-G pullout to return to pattern altitude for the next delivery. A 4-G pullout is no big deal. Hell, I'd even managed to perform a 4-G pullout over Hanoi when my balls were getting crushed between my body and my harness! But today, I was having a real problem tolerating G-forces.

I kept blacking out during the pull-outs. I wouldn't lose consciousness, I just lost vision for a few seconds under high G-loading. But losing vision, even for a very short period of time, is a bad thing. Really bad. In the bombing pattern, I needed to maintain my position over the ground and keep visual separation from the other airplanes in the flight. This was not working out well at all.

To make matters worse, this was supposed to be my qualification mission for the air-to-ground DOC. I was already qualified in air-to-air, and getting this final qualification would make me Combat Ready. But I would need good bombs, and I wasn't getting them.

On the gunnery range, we would attempt to get our practice bombs directly on the target, a pyramid-shaped structure about six feet across at the center of the bombing circle. Each practice bomb would emit a small puff of smoke when it hit the ground, and the Range Control Officer and his assistant, stationed in two towers a few hundred feet apart, would point their calibrated tripod-mounted binoculars at the smoke and triangulate their results to determine the distance from the target for each bomb delivery. The results would be given in distance and azimuth relative to the run-in direction, such as "10 feet at six o'clock". The Range Control Officer would record the results and give us our scores after each delivery.

My deliveries were shitty. Certainly not good enough to meet qualification standards. It was embarrassing and humiliating. Here I was, having just returned from doing this for a living in actual combat, and I couldn't even get my bombs on target when no one was shooting at me. I already knew I hadn't met qualification standards before we even left the range. The only bright spot in the whole mission was that my last bomb was a "shack", a direct hit. So I ended on a high note.

I felt totally drained all the way back to CCK. My formation flying was getting sloppy, and I handed the airplane over to my back-seater, Johnny Johnson, for a while. Johnny really loved to get stick time, so he thought I was being nice to him. Actually, I was just trying to keep from dinging a wingtip with flight lead. I took the airplane again as we entered Initial.

We had the standard five-second break for a pitch-out into a 60-degree bank, an easy 2-G load factor in the pull. And I was blacking out! This was not good at all. I grunted as I performed the M-1 maneuver, and said, "Hey, Johnny, take the airplane for a second."

Johnny gladly flew the airplane around the pattern, and on downwind I regained my vision and took the airplane again. I dropped approach flaps, extended the gear and selected final flaps as I turned base. I kept the airplane on profile, and the aural Angle of Attack tone in my headset informed me that I was on speed. I had a good, firm touchdown, and lowered the nose for the roll out.

"Drag chute, Hamfist, drag chute!" Johnny was yelling in the headset.

Shit! I'd flown over 500 hours in the F-4, and had never before forgotten to deploy the drag chute on landing. I reached over, double-checked that I had the correct handle, and deployed the drag chute. We cleared the runway, went to the de-arm area, and then taxied to parking. As we parked, I shut down the engines, performed the post-flight checklist, and raised the canopy.

Sergeant Adams quickly put the ladder on the left canopy rail and climbed up to insert the pins in my ejection seat.

"Sir! Are you okay?"

I didn't respond. I was fumbling with my oxygen mask, trying to disconnect it so I could remove my helmet, and my fingers weren't working. Finally, I just leaned back in the seat and shut my eyes. I would rest for a second or two until I got up enough energy to finish unstrapping. Just a second or two.

The next thing I knew, emergency responders from the Fire Department were removing me from the cockpit and handing me over to the medics in the waiting ambulance.

As I saw my airplane recede into the distance through the rear window of the ambulance, I had the sick feeling that I would never again strap on a Phantom.

12

May 12, 1973

The Flight Surgeon stood at the foot of my bed, looking at the chart that had the results of my blood tests.

"Been doing a lot of kissing lately?" he smiled.

"Not really," I answered, "Why?"

"I was just pulling your leg, Hamilton. You have Mononucleosis. Back in the old days, when I was in med school, we used to call that the Kissing Disease. Your blood pressure is dangerously low, your sub-mandible glands are grossly swollen, and your spleen is really enlarged."

"Well if it's not kissing, what causes it?"

"You probably were burning the candle at both ends and weakened your immune system, making you susceptible to the Epstein-Barr virus."

"What do I take for it?"

"There's no medicine for it. Bed rest. That's it. You need to rest up for at least a week, preferably two."

"So I'll be able to fly again in two weeks?"

"Oh, no way. You'll be DNIF for at least two months."

Shit. This was bad. DNIF was Duty Not Involving Flying, such as administrative duties around the squadron. I'd probably end up pulling RSO a lot. And it would take me an extra two months to get Combat Ready. This would really look bad for my application for Fighter Weapons School.

The USAF Fighter Weapons School, at Nellis Air Force Base in Nevada, was the most highly selective course a fighter pilot could attend. Only the best of the best got to go, and normally there was only one slot per year for each wing. Taking four months to get Combat Ready would be the kiss of death for any selection hopes I had. There were a ton of guys in the two squadrons in our wing who wanted to attend Fighter Weapons School, and none of them had taken excessive time to qualify.

I wanted to argue with the Flight Surgeon, but I just didn't have the energy. After he left my room, I shut my eyes and went to sleep.

I slept for pretty much the next two days. When I finally opened my eyes, I thought I was dreaming. Sam was sitting next to my bed. And she looked *huge*.

"Am I dreaming again, or is that you?"

"It's me, Ham," she smiled, as she leaned over and kissed me. "I've been here for two hours, and you were totally out. You didn't move a muscle. At first I thought you were in a coma."

"Well, this mono really knocked me out, but seeing you here has me feeling better already."

Then I realized I had just kissed her. I rang the call button, and the nurse quickly arrived.

"My wife just kissed me. On the lips! Is she going to get mono? Is the baby going to be okay?"

"Relax, Captain. Your wife will be fine, as long as she doesn't do anything to weaken her immunity." She glanced at Sam. "It looks to me like there's a good two months until delivery. After the baby comes home is when you'll both be worn out."

"I'm really sorry, Sam," I said, "I guess I was working too hard. I was really looking forward to you coming here. I got us a reservation at a great hotel downtown."

"I know, Ham. I'm already checked in. Nice place." She looked at the nurse. "Is he receiving any kind of special medication, or IV?"

"No, just plenty of bed rest."

Sam looked at me. "I'll be back in a minute, Honey. I want to talk to your doctor."

After about ten minutes, Sam and the Flight Surgeon entered my room.

"You have a very persuasive wife, Hamilton," he smiled, "I think it's in the best interest of everyone involved if you vacate the hospital and get your bed rest at the Grand Hotel. Needs of the service."

I may not have had much energy up to that point, but I didn't need any help getting dressed and getting my ass out of that hospital as fast as I could. We took a taxi to the Grand Hotel, and we both got out of our clothes and climbed into the gigantic bed.

"The doctor said to take it easy, honey," she said. "Are you sure you're going to be up to having sex?"

"I may be a little sick, but I'm not dead! What about you? Is it okay to have sex this close to delivery?"

"My gynecologist said there would be no problem. Unless you're planning on getting rough," she laughed.

"Don't worry. I'll be gentle."

I was gentle. And I proved I wasn't dead.

13

May 26, 1973

That week went by quickly, too quickly. I felt stronger every day, and after about three days I started going for short walks around town with Sam. We would go out for an hour or two, then I'd get back in bed and rest. Having Sam there with me was the best medicine I could have hoped for.

When we went for walks, Sam was able to introduce me to many of the shops and restaurants that didn't normally cater to Americans, because their signs were written in Chinese. Since Japanese written characters are similar to Chinese, she was able to read all of the signs and announcements. It was pretty funny when we would enter a store and the sales people would try to talk to her in Chinese. Typically, the owners couldn't speak English, and they would end up communicating with Sam by writing.

After Sam left at the end of the week, I went back to my room at the BOQ, and stayed in bed most of the time for the next week. I went to the squadron for a few hours each day to take care of my duties at Life Support, and worked up to about four hours a day.

When I got back to the squadron, I heard about an event that had occurred while I was in the hospital. Our sister squadron had been scheduled for the Dawn Patrol and several early morning gunnery missions. It turned out that every mission had been canceled due to aircraft non-availability. Total MND. Every one. Maintenance was *really* on its ass.

Well, the crews were pissed, and I couldn't blame them. They had gotten up early, sometimes 0300 hours, briefed their missions, retrieved their equipment from Life Support, walked out to their airplanes and *then* found out that they were a no-go. I would've been pissed, too. Following the MND, the crews did what any self-respecting fighter jocks would do. They went to the bar, bitched, told war stories, and got shit-faced drunk. They stayed there all day.

By 1900 hours, most of them were using the "Little People's Bar", the foot rest at the bottom of the bar, to hold their drinks. They were well past blasted. And, as the witching hour – 1900 – struck, the bartender made his usual announcement.

"Gentlemen," he said, in Chinese-accented English, "It's 1900 hours. No flight suits are allowed in the club."

It wouldn't be hard to predict what happened next. The jocks staggered to their feet, unzipped their flight suits, and stood there with their flight suits around their ankles. And then they started to get rowdy.

There had been friction between the F-4 drivers and the C-130 permanent-party crews ever since the wing had arrived. The C-130s owned the base, and they never stopped letting us know it. We were a tenant unit, visitors, red-head step-children. Everything on base revolved around the "Herkeys," the nickname for the C-130 Lockheed Hercules. The fighter jocks quickly transformed the nickname to "Turkeys".

Just as the jocks were stripping to their skivvies, the C-130 Wing Commander entered the O'Club, escorting a visiting General. They apparently had just returned from the golf course, and the Wing Commander was wearing a Hawaiian shirt and casual pants. As soon as he heard the commotion in the bar, he rushed in.

"What's going on here?" he demanded.

A young Lieutenant went up to him, looked him in the eye, and swayed back and forth.

"You must be pretty fucking stupid if you can't see what's going on here."

"Do you know who I am?" the Colonel bellowed.

"No. Who are you?"

"I'm the Wing Commander!" he yelled, veins popping out of his neck.

The Lieutenant squinted and looked him over,

rocking back and forth.

"Oh. You're the *Turkey* Wing Commander!"

Things were degenerating rapidly. The Wing Commander got on his "brick" hand-held radio and called for the Air Police. A few of the jocks realized that things were going south quickly, and pulled up their flight suits and left the club. They even put on their scarves and rolled down their flight suit sleeves. They looked totally proper as the Air Police arrived, sirens blazing.

The sky cops looked at the exiting pilots. "What's going on in there?"

"There's some guy in a Hawaiian shirt," answered one of the pilots, "causing a ruckus and tearing the place up."

As the sky cops entered the Club, the exiting pilots made a hasty retreat.

By dawn the next day, the shit had totally hit the fan. The Commander of our sister squadron had been fired, and was already off the island. He hadn't even been at the club. He was a tea-totaler, and had been in his room the whole time, oblivious to what had been transpiring. His replacement, a Lieutenant Colonel from Fifth Air Force Headquarters, was already on his way from Yokota. Everyone in the squadron received an RBI – Reply By Indorsement – a letter that required a response, in which the recipient of the letter had to explain what he had been doing the night of the event. Everyone who had been in the bar received an Article 15, a military punishment that effectively destroyed any chance of promotion. And, a few days later General McKenzie, the Pacific Air Forces Commander, announced that the 18th Tactical Fighter Wing could no longer perform formation takeoffs.

"If those bastards can't keep their flight suits on," he supposedly said, "they sure as shit can't do formation takeoffs."

I, of course, had the perfect alibi. I was in the hospital.

Most of the other guys in my squadron were also out of the woods. They had all been downtown, chasing pussy at the Dirty Dozen.

14

May 27, 1973

The Wing had a stand-down. No flying at all, just meetings all day.

First, we all assembled in the base theater, where our Wing Commander gave us an ass-chewing. He had flown in from Kadena, in an RF-4, that morning, and would be flying back as soon as he was finished reaming us out.

He expounded on how officers should behave, how he wouldn't tolerate any more embarrassing events, and how disappointed he was with us. And he told us we'd better get our families to behave, also. There was entirely too much drug use on the part of the teenagers whose fathers were deployed to CCK. And wives were having a melt-down. One of them had found his home telephone number, and had personally called him as she attempted suicide.

"You better get your families in line. I won't put up with any more of this unprofessional, irresponsible behavior. Some day you're all going to look back on this deployment as the best time of your life."

That General really had his finger on the pulse of the Wing. *Not*.

After we left the base theater, both squadrons had separate meetings at their mass briefing rooms. As usual, Cocktail was nowhere in sight. Lieutenant Colonel Milner was conducting our meeting. With no one in our squadron on the Wing Commander's current shit list, he had a look like the cat that ate the canary.

"I want to commend you all for the way you represented our squadron," he announced.

He proceeded to discuss some operational issues, schedules, and flight procedures. Then he announced the need for some volunteers for additional duties.

"We need someone to volunteer for Admin Officer, because Captain Dolan is going to DEROS in another month. And we need someone to help Lieutenant Murphy with the snack bar."

He paused, looked around the room until he made eye contact with me, and continued, "And we need a volunteer to be Life Support Officer... Hancock," he smiled wickedly, "you're going to Wing O&T."

15

May 27, 1973

I thought back to a conversation I'd had with Duke shortly after I had arrived at CCK.

"Hamfist," Duke asked, "do you have your gates met?"

The "gates" were artificial thresholds of years of service and hours of flying time, established to designate pilots who could be utilized for non-flying duties. Basically, if a pilot was on track to meet the requirements of the Senior Pilot aeronautical award, he was deemed to have met his gates. To receive Senior Pilot wings, the pilot had to have accumulated 2000 hours flying time and have been rated for at least seven years.

I was well short of seven years of rated time, but I had almost 1500 hours already, and had over 500 hours in the F-4. The gates for fighter units were established at 1000 hours total time and 450 hours of fighter time. Anyone who had that experience level was eligible to be assigned to a nonflying position. Guys with less experience were guaranteed they would stay in the cockpit.

"I guess I do. Why do you ask?"

"I saw a notice on the squadron bulletin board that Wing is looking for Captains who have met their gates for some staff jobs. Command Post and O&T – the Operations and Training Division. They prefer volunteers."

"Who the hell would volunteer?"

"Probably senior Captains who are bucking for Major below the zone. A staff job is considered a necessity if you want early promotion."

"I wouldn't mind making Major early," I said, "but I'm not ready to leave operational flying. Do the staff guys get much flying?"

"They fly as attached pilots, get minimum time, and they don't maintain Combat Ready status. A few intercepts a month, maybe a range ride or two. But they still fly the F-4."

I thought about my prospects for getting to Fighter Weapons School if I volunteered for a staff job, and immediately discounted it. Unless I was assigned to the Wing Weapons Division, getting a staff job would be the end of my quest for Weapons School. Of course, the mono took care of that a month later.

The bitch of it was, if I'd had about 50 hours less F-4 time, I wouldn't have been eligible for a staff job, since the minimum was 450 hours of fighter time. But, I figured, at least I'd still get to fly the F-4 as a staff pilot, as soon as I was off DNIF.

I couldn't have been more wrong.

16

May 28, 1973

Wing Operations and Training Division was where fighter pilot careers went to die. O&T had no single specific mission. Instead, in addition to monitoring flight training activities, it was a catch-all cats and dogs operation that consisted of all of the go-fer jobs that Wing Plans Section didn't handle. The office was staffed by three Majors – Navigators – who were really on the ball, and three pilots, all ROAD – Retired On Active Duty – Majors.

I had been instructed to leave CCK and report to Wing Headquarters, back at Kadena. I checked into the BOQ – Bachelor Officer Quarters – and then showed up at Wing O&T to the surprised look of the Chief of the section, a Lieutenant Colonel RF-4 pilot.

"We didn't expect to get anyone for another six months," he said, extending his hand. "I'm Ron Basset. Most people call me Ron Recce."

Recce was the abbreviation for Reconnaissance, the mission of the RF-4. Ron had flown recce his entire career, first in RF-101s, then in RF-4s. He had more recce time than any other pilot in the Air Force. And he wanted me to call him Ron.

"Sir," I said, "I'm not really comfortable calling you by your first name."

"Well then, Ham, you're going to be talking to yourself a lot, because that's what I answer to."

"Yes, sir. I mean, okay, Ron."

He smiled.

At his assignment prior to coming to Kadena, Ron had been the Ops Officer of an RF-4 training squadron at Shaw Air Force Base, back in the States. He had been assigned to Kadena to replace the outgoing RF-4 Squadron Commander, who was due to DEROS just as Ron would be arriving. Ron already had 21 years of service, and had been planning to retire. But the prospects of becoming a Squadron Commander had been too good to pass up, so he accepted the overseas position at Kadena, a three-year assignment.

But Ron got screwed. While he was en route to Kadena, a local Lieutenant Colonel, the RF-4 Ops Officer, somehow prevailed upon the powers that be and got himself installed as the new Squadron Commander. When Ron arrived on the island, around the same time I got there, he was out of a job. He got shuttled off to become the Chief of the Operations and Training Division.

To say he was pissed would be an understatement. But he was pragmatic. He knew he was stuck overseas for the next 36 months. So he decided he was going to make the best of a bad deal. He was going to just enjoy himself at Kadena. He wasn't bucking for promotion to Colonel, so he decided to do the minimum necessary work and let the worker bees, and the ROAD Majors, run the shop. And he was going to fly his ass off.

When he lost the Squadron Commander position, Ron went up to the Wing Commander and made him an offer he couldn't refuse. He cited Title 10 of the United States Code, which specified that the senior pilot would be designated Squadron Commander. Ron was senior to the Lieutenant Colonel who had assumed command of the recce squadron. He told the Wing Commander he was willing to withdraw his request for an Inspector General investigation and his planned complaint to his Congressman if he could fly with the recce squadron like a normal jock and maintain Combat Ready status in the recce mission. The Wing Commander was no idiot. What he had done, taking command away from Ron, was illegal as hell. He gave Ron what he wanted.

And Ron flew a lot. When he was in the office, which wasn't too often, he didn't do much, other than divide up the work assignments to the Navs and to me. If there was a project that wasn't important, he'd shuttle it off to one of the ROAD Majors.

Ron wasn't crazy about staff work, so he decided

he would make the job as easy on himself as he could. When a tasking came to his office in the way of any kind of official letter, he simply dropped it in the bottom drawer of his desk.

"If it's important," he announced, "they'll send a follow-up letter. The rest of the junk," he proudly pointed to his overstuffed drawer, "will die a natural death."

Actually, I discovered, it wasn't such a bad way to run the office. There were a lot of projects that were total bullshit, and really didn't warrant any effort. The downside, of course, was that when an important project missed a deadline, we were already a week behind schedule in completing it.

I quickly discovered that the ROAD Majors were pretty worthless. One Major, nicknamed Flip, was constantly leaving the office early, supposedly because he was feeling ill. More than once, though, he was spotted on the Kadena golf course after leaving work early.

When Flip was around, he did as little work as he could. One of the O&T duties was serving as OPR – Office of Primary Responsibility – for any suggestions submitted through the Air Force Suggestion Program that pertained to Operations.

"Here's the way to handle suggestions that come to us for evaluation," Flip told me, "We don't have the authority to approve most suggestions. That would come from higher headquarters. So what I do is figure out a way to deny it. That way I don't have to follow up on it like I would if I had sent it up to higher headquarters."

I thought back to all of the suggestions I had submitted in my previous assignment. I had made a lot of money, and had gotten a lot of career mileage, from those suggestions. If the Suggestion Program monitors at Ubon had operated the way Flip did, I would have been screwed. I didn't want that to happen to the jocks at Kadena.

"Hey, Flip, I'd like to manage the Suggestion Program."

"Okay, Hamilton, if you want it, you got it."

The three ROAD Majors were all in the Sanctuary, past the eighteen-year point in their careers. That meant they were guaranteed they would make it to 20 years for their retirements. They couldn't be separated from the Air Force against their will, like junior officers could. With junior officers, if there was a surplus of officers, the Air Force could declare a Reduction In Force – RIF – and separate the officers at any time. When a Lieutenant or Captain got RIF'd, he would usually get RIF pay, a few months' salary. But our ROAD Majors were immune to being RIF'd, and they knew it.

The ROAD Majors refused to go TDY to CCK. The

O&T Division had an officer at CCK at all times, to manage the training activities of the two fighter squadrons. So, when the ROAD Majors didn't pull their share of TDY, the rest of us had to take up the slack. We would go TDY to CCK for one month at a time, which was nothing compared to what the fighter jocks had to put up with.

Getting assigned to O&T was a good deal for me in one respect. I didn't need to worry about missing Sam's delivery.

"Listen," Ron said, "I'm signing this Military Leave Request right now, so if I'm out flying and you need to take leave on short notice, here it is in my desk. You go when you need to go."

"Thank you, Ron."

"You're welcome. Remember, family is the most important thing, it takes priority over everything else. You do whatever you need to do to be there when your son or daughter is born. If you're not there, you'll regret it your whole life."

Ron always kept his office, and his desk, unlocked.

I appreciated that.

17

June 1, 1973

I started learning the ropes at Wing O&T. I was in totally unfamiliar territory wearing my blue uniform and showing up every morning at 0730. Up until this time, throughout my career I had always been wearing a flight suit, and had been operating on "flex time", showing up at 0300, 0400, whenever I was scheduled. And it usually changed every day. I liked the variety. Now, I would have a predictable schedule, and I was really worried that it would quickly get boring.

Every morning there was a staff meeting with the Wing Director of Operations. The meeting usually started at 0800, and every department with inputs to Operations had a representative in attendance. There were attendees from Maintenance, Logistics, each fighter squadron, Plans, and, of course, O&T. Because the fighter squadrons were all TDY, Sergeant Molloy was their representative.

Ron wanted each of us to take turns attending the staff meetings. The ROAD Majors simply said they weren't interested in participating, and there wasn't much Ron could do to force them. So the Navigators and I took turns attending.

Every attendee had to be ready to answer any questions that arose, which usually centered around the previous day's flying activities. For the O&T Division, there were a lot of reports to digest before the daily staff meeting, so whoever was going to attend the meeting usually came to work at 0600 or sooner, to be totally prepared.

The first time I attended a meeting I was really a fish out of water. At one point, the DO looked in my direction.

"What were the results of the Qualification mission for the new pilot," he looked down at his steno pad, "that would be Captain Andrews?"

I knew that there had been a mission to the gunnery range the previous day, and I knew that the FNG, Captain Andrews, had been in the flight. But I had no idea if he had qualified for Combat Ready status. And I didn't even know where to find the information. I looked through the sheaf of reports on my lap and drew a blank. I glanced over at Sergeant Molloy, and received a blank look. I squirmed in my seat.

"I don't have that information right now, sir. I'll get it to your office as soon as we finish up here."

He nodded. I wasn't sure if he was satisfied with my answer, or if he was sizing me up and concluding I was just like the ROAD Majors.

As soon as the meeting ended, I rushed back to my office and went up to Bill Steers, one of the Navigator Majors, who had become my mentor at O&T.

"Bill, how do I find the information on Captain Andrews's Qual ride yesterday?"

Bill picked up a clipboard with a ream of teletype messages.

"Here you go," he pointed to a line in the teletype message, "this is how we decode the message."

Bill spent the next fifteen minutes explaining what all the previously indecipherable segments of an Air Force message meant. It would take some adjusting, but I was starting to see the light. And I was able to find the information for the DO. I looked at the report, then hurried to the DO's office.

Amy, the DO's secretary, was in the outer office. We had been introduced when I began my assignment to O&T, but I hadn't really had any contact with her until now.

"Good morning, Amy. Colonel Wilson had asked me for some information about yesterday's range mission, and I have the answer for him."

"Oh, you must mean the Qualification mission for Captain Andrews."

She sure didn't miss a thing. I nodded.

"Just a second," she said, disappearing into the inner office. Shortly she reappeared. "Colonel Wilson will see you now."

"Thank you, Amy."

I entered the DO's office, stood at attention, and saluted. Colonel Wilson returned my salute.

"Relax, Ham. When you come into my office to give me information I've asked for, there's no need to report and salute. If we did that, we'd be saluting all day." He paused. "So, how did Andrews do?"

"Sir, he qualified on the range mission, and is now Combat Ready in all three DOCs."

"Thanks, Ham. I'll let you know if I need any more information."

"Yes sir."

I turned to leave his office. As I got to the door, Colonel Wilson called to me.

"Ham, any idea how his bombs were? What kind of CEA?"

The CEA is the Circular Error Average, which is the average, in feet, of all the bomb deliveries for a pilot on any particular mission. For example, if he had a 20-foot miss and a 30-foot miss on two deliveries, he would have a CEA of 25 feet.

There was another statistic that was used as a measure of fighter pilot accuracy, the CEP. The CEP is the Circular Error Probable, which is the smallest circular error that encompasses 50 percent of all the pilot's deliveries. If the pilot, for example, had one 10-foot miss and a 100-foot miss, his CEP would be 10 feet.

"Sir, Captain Andrews had a CEA of 55 feet."

Colonel Wilson looked satisfied. "Any idea of his CEP?"

I could see he was evaluating me, to see how thorough I was in my research.

"His CEP was 22 feet, sir."

"Thank you, Ham. Good job."

I had passed the DO's first test.

18

June 1, 1973

Bill spent the rest of the day explaining pretty much everything we would be doing in O&T, and where I would need to go for additional information. One of our duties was managing the scheduling of the Ie Shima bombing range, off the coast of Okinawa.

The 18th TFW managed the range, but there were a lot of users, such as the Navy, the Marines, and some of the fighter units at bases in Korea. So O&T was the one-stop center for assigning range times.

This actually required quite a bit of coordination. If the range was already reserved for all the daytime slots except 1500, we needed to coordinate with flight scheduling to ensure that the range mission for the 18th TFW would be scheduled for a 1330 takeoff. That assumed an en route flight time of an hour 30 minutes to get from CCK to the range. Then we would need to coordinate for a post-mission in-flight refueling at 1545, assuming a range exit at 1530 and 15 minutes to get to the refueling rendezvous point.

Coordinating refueling required calling the KC-135 Refueling Squadron, which was also located at Kadena.

It usually took several phone calls to make sure there was a tanker aircraft available, with the available fuel load, and that the airspace required for the refueling track was not reserved for any other activity. Refueling airspace reservations required a call to PACAF – Pacific Air Forces — headquarters. And since PACAF Headquarters was located in Hawaii, six hours ahead of Kadena, all communication with them had to occur during the morning in Kadena.

And, of course, if any of these scheduled times conflicted, we needed to start all over again. Maybe we'd need to call the Marines and see if we could trade time slots at Ie Shima. This was really, really different from anything I had done before!

O&T also scheduled entry into the Warning Areas, which were used for live-fire activities. Again, there were a lot of users, and they all came to O&T for reservations.

Then, we had counterparts at the Japan Air Self-Defense Force fighter squadron, located at Naha Air Base, at the south end of Okinawa. The JASDF had a variety of fighter aircraft, and we would periodically perform joint exercises with them. These exercises were highly orchestrated events, and the Wing Weapons Section handled the implementation of the exercises. Our job at O&T was to interface with our contemporaries at the JASDF squadron to make sure the resources were available at the scheduled time.

By the end of the day, I felt totally spent. I couldn't wait to get off DNIF status, so I could at least break up my work schedule by getting back to flying the F-4.

I was in for an unpleasant surprise.

19

June 15, 1973

I had made really good progress on my PME, having just completed the final section of Air Command and Staff College. Now that I had gotten into the habit of studying every night, I decided to visit the Base Education Office to see what other course options there were. I had heard that the Industrial College of the Armed Forces offered a correspondence course, and thought it would really look good on my record. And I'd heard it was a really good course, with actual hardbound books, unlike the paperbacks I'd received for Air Command and Staff College.

"Hi," I said to Mary, the secretary at the Education Office, "how do I sign up for ICAF?"

"I'm sorry, sir, but you're not eligible. It's reserved for Field Grade officers, Majors and above."

I think the disappointment clearly showed on my face.

"Captain," she continued, "have you considered working on your Master's Degree?"

Although I knew there were college course offered

through the Education Office, I hadn't been aware that it was possible to get a Master's Degree on base.

"What kind of Master's do you offer?"

"Actually, we don't offer it, we just help manage it. The courses are offered through the University of Southern California. You can get a Master's in Education or Systems Management." She paused. "I'm not supposed to tell you this, but I recommend Systems Management. I got my Master's in Education, and the only job I could get was as a secretary here in the Education Office."

"Okay, how do I sign up for Systems Management?"

Mary proceeded to help me fill out the forms to register for my first course, and to apply for Tuition Assistance. The TA Program allowed me to take my courses at almost no cost. The Air Force would pick up the cost of tuition, while I would be responsible for the rest of the expenses, such as purchasing textbooks.

The really neat thing about the courses were that they were not sequential – no course was a prerequisite for any other course. That way, a student could start any time a new course began. My timing was perfect – there would be a course starting the next Monday.

I wasn't sure what to expect when I showed up for class, which began at 1800 and ran until 2300, twice a week for ten weeks. My first course was Human Factors, which promised to be really interesting. A lot of the examples involved aircraft cockpits, and about half of the other students were pilots.

The instructor was from the University, and had volunteered to be a "traveling professor" for a year, spending three months at each of four bases in Asia. He had a PhD in Physics, and had lots of actual experience in industry. I could see I would learn a lot.

This class was the instructor's first foray into the Air Force environment, and he didn't really understand how TDY assignments affected our schedules.

"I will be taking attendance," he said, "and, if you miss two classes, you will drop one grade, from an A to a B as your best grade. If you miss two more classes, that will drop you an additional grade." He paused. "You know, you're required to have at least a B average to graduate, so if you get a C, you'll need an A to offset that. So I suggest you don't miss any classes."

I didn't like what I was hearing.

"Professor," I said, "do you realize that many of us will be required to miss classes due to TDY assignments? We may end up missing three or more classes due to our military duties."

"What's TDY?"

I could see this professor hadn't been around military people before.

"It's Temporary Duty, where we're sent to another base for duty. We're serving in the military, and shouldn't be penalized for doing our jobs."

"Well, then, Mr. Hancock, what do you suggest?"

He knew my name because we had written our names on cardboard name tags folded on our desks.

"If we need to miss class, how about if we write a paper or some other assignment that demonstrates that we have learned the material for that lesson?"

"Very compelling idea," he replied. He paused for a moment. "I will need a 10-page paper for every class attendance you miss. Will that work?"

"Yes, sir. I think that will work out."

"One more thing, Mr. Hancock," he continued, "I'm not really used to being around military people. My name is Jack, not Sir."

"Got it, Jack."

I could see this was going to work out just fine.

20

July 1, 1973

I received a call at the office. It was Tom, Sam's dad.

"Ham, it's time. Sam is having intermittent contractions, and the doctor wants her in the hospital. He said it will probably be a couple of days until she delivers, but he wants her in bed and under supervision. I think you should get here as soon as you can."

As usual, Ron was out flying. I went to his office, grabbed the signed Leave Request and filled it in. I left a copy on his desk, along with a short note thanking him and telling him how to get in contact with me. Then I called Don Watson, at the MAC Command Post.

"Don, this is Ham. Sam is going into labor. Are there any flights heading to Yokota in the next few hours?"

"How soon can you get down to Base Ops?"

"I can get there in ten minutes."

"Stand by, Ham," Major Watson said. In the background I heard him talking on the radio to a MAC flight.

"Flight 1408, Command Post. Hold your position. We have a high-priority courier that needs to get on your flight. ETA ten minutes."

I heard the radio crackle, "Roger, Command Post. Standing by."

He got back on the phone.

"Get down here ASAP, Ham. There's a C-141 waiting for you."

"Thank you, Don. I'm on my way."

I got in my car and made great time to Base Ops. I had packed a small bag with about a week's supply of clothing and had put it in my trunk several days earlier. When I got to Base Ops, I pulled into the parking lot, grabbed my bag and ran to the terminal.

Don was waiting at the terminal entrance. As soon as he saw me, he grabbed my bag and said, "Follow me."

We went out to a blue Air Force truck that was parked at the curb, and he drove me onto the flight line. As he drove, he was calling Ground Control on his hand-held radio, getting clearance to proceed to the waiting Starlifter.

Our truck screeched to a halt at the front entrance

of the airplane. The Loadmaster was waiting by the entrance stairs.

"Come this way, sir."

I followed him onto the airplane, stopping to turn to silently mouth "Thanks" to Don. The Loadmaster escorted me to a jump seat in the cockpit, and, after our initial introductions, I sat in silence during a flight that seemed to take forever.

When we pulled up to the remote parking spot at Yokota, there was a staff car waiting for me. Good old Don.

The driver delivered me to the base hospital at about 1800 hours. When I arrived at the main entrance, Tom and Miyako were waiting for me. It was really great to see them again. We quickly embraced.

"Come on, Ham," Tom said, "I'll show you to Sam's room."

We went up to the third floor, and Tom led me into Room 304.

Sam looked absolutely radiant. Other than her large, no, *huge*, stomach, she looked exactly like the first time I met her, when I had been instantly enchanted by her.

She reached out from her bed to hug me.

"I am so anxious to get this show on the road," she said, "The doctor insisted that I stay in bed until delivery, and I would just as soon be up and about."

"Well, Honey, I'm sure the doctor knows what's best," I said, as I kissed her and gently, very gently, hugged her.

"I know," she responded, "I'm just anxious to meet little what's-his-name."

21

July 3, 1973

It was great to finally have some time, in person, with Sam. It had been hard to have any kind of serious extended conversation on the autovon. I knew I was using a secure telephone line, and no one would be listening, but I hadn't been given unlimited talk time at the CCK Command Post like I'd had at Kadena. And using the MARS line – Military Affiliate Radio Station – was out of the question, since there was no privacy at all using MARS. In addition to the radio operators at each end of the line, there was normally a long line of GIs waiting to make calls listening over the loudspeaker in the room on every MARS call.

I had been able to get an autovon call to Sam about once a week while I was at CCK. We would talk for about 20 minutes, but it wasn't anything like having a face-to-face conversation. I had gotten Sam pregnant when she was TDY to Ubon, where I had been based during Operation Linebacker, and we hadn't really had much of an opportunity to collaborate on a name for our child.

I had bought two copies of a book of baby names at the CCK Base Exchange book store, sent one to Sam, and we started with the letter A and went all the way through the book over the course of two months. It seemed like most of the names were either ethnic or outdated. I just couldn't picture our son being named Nicodemus Hancock.

There were a couple of names that, for me, were show-stoppers. I really wasn't crazy about the name Hamilton. For starters, the whole time I was growing up, when teachers would initially see my name on a class roster, they would think it was my last name. And I thought it was a bit too self-serving to name my son, if I had one, after myself. I wanted him to be able to strike out on his own, not live in his father's shadow.

And I didn't want him or her to have any artsy-fartsy name, especially one with a weird spelling. If our daughter was going to be named Jacqueline, it would be the normal spelling, not Jacklyn or some other off-the-wall variation.

And I wanted our children to have monikers with acceptable variations, in case they weren't crazy about their official names. James could morph into Jim or Jimmy, Jonathan could become John or Johnny or Jack, Stephen could be Steve or Stevie.

Now we were finally together, and we could discuss names at a more leisurely pace. Complicating the naming ritual was the fact that we had no idea what sex our child would be. I had heard about a procedure that would enable us to know the sex in advance, called amniocentesis.

I asked Sam what she thought of the idea. She would have none of that.

"First of all, no matter what they say, it probably entails some risk to the baby. And regardless of what the tests show, the baby's sex is already determined, and won't change. Let's allow ourselves to be surprised," she said.

"Besides," she continued, "I've been carrying our child ten inches under my heart for the past nine months. He, or maybe she, has been communicating with me for quite a while. I think he-she will tell me his-her name when the time comes."

"Okay, but no Junior, okay?"

"Okay, no Junior," she smiled.

22

July 3, 1973

Tom and I were alone in his apartment while Miyako was holding down the fort at the hospital.

"Have the two of you come close to selecting a name?" Tom asked.

"Not really. I had been thinking of the name June if it was a girl and if she was born last month. I really like the name Samantha, but that's already taken," I smiled. "I definitely don't want my son to be a Junior. I'm not crazy about the name Hamilton, and I think it's too egotistical to be a Junior, anyway."

"Did Sam tell you her preferences?"

"She has some names she's partial to, but we never got enough time together to have an extended conversation. We talked a little today, but didn't come to any definite conclusions."

"I guess you know my daughter can be stubborn when she wants to be."

"So I've discovered," I replied, "but it's not over until the fat lady sings."

"Funny you should use that expression," Tom remarked. "Do you know where that originated?"

"No," I answered. I suspected I was about to find out.

Tom got up from his chair and walked over to the stereo console. He flipped through the LP records that were stacked vertically in the compartment on the left side of the cabinet, and found what he was looking for. He held the album reverently, and carefully handed it to me. There was a black-and-white photograph on the cover, a head shot of an overweight lady.

"Do you know who this is?" he asked, gently retrieving the album.

"No," I answered, "I don't think so. Wait a minute… is that Kate Smith?"

"Very good. Not many people your age recognize her."

" I remember my mom used to watch her show on television when I was a kid."

"She had a television show in the 50s. But she had a radio show in the thirties. Back then I was in college in New York," Tom said.

"What school?" I interrupted.

"Cooper Union. There was no tuition cost.

Everyone there was on a scholarship. I didn't have much money at the time. It was during the depression. I was barely able to eat on the salary I made driving a hack."

Tom smiled when he saw the shocked look on my face. For some reason, I had pictured him as always having been wealthy. And certainly not a taxi driver.

"When I had time off, for entertainment, I would stand outside the WABC studios to see if I could get in to see the Kate Smith Hour for free. It was a great show. Henny Youngman, Abbott and Costello, lots of great guests. Plus Kate, who could really belt out a song."

"Anyway," he continued, "I had the day off on Armistice Day, 1938. That was twenty years to the day after World War I ended. You know, The War To End All Wars." He gave a wry smile. "There were no classes, and the cab company didn't have any work for me. I got dressed up in my one and only suit and stood outside the studio entrance. It was a cold day, and a long wait. I guess because of the way I was dressed, I was the first one they let in. I sat right in the front row of the audience."

As he was speaking, Tom was carefully placing the record onto the turntable. He turned on the stereo and gently lowered the needle onto the record. Then he grabbed a box of tissues and sat down next to me.

"This was the first time she ever sang this song," he said, as the as the scratching sound ended and the music began.

After a brief introduction with a reference to the storm clouds forming over Europe, Kate sang *God Bless America*. I was transfixed.

When the song ended, Tom grabbed a tissue and handed the box to me.

"I think I got a speck of dust in my eye," he smiled.

"Me too," I answered, as I grabbed a tissue.

"Kate Smith was nothing to look at. Nothing compared to Marilyn Monroe and the other stars. But she was on radio, so her looks didn't matter. After that performance, that song became her trademark. She started and ended every show with it. It became hers."

"And that," Tom said, "is where the expression 'It's not over until the fat lady sings' came from. Like Paul Harvey says, 'now you know the *rest* of the story'."

"In 1960," he continued, "after I was pretty well established, I was in New York on business. I was having lunch at the Four Seasons, and looked over and there was Kate Smith, a few tables away."

He paused.

"You know, I've met a lot of big shots, and I am not what you would call star-struck. But I went over to her table and, for a minute, I was a young college kid again.

And I told her that I had been in her audience that Armistice Day. And how I often thought of that performance when I was overseas, during the war. She confided to me that, right after she sang it, she called Irving Berlin and told him he had written the next national anthem. She was so gracious. A real lady."

Tom turned over the record sleeve, and showed me where she had autographed the album: *To Tom Marcos. Thank you for your service. God bless America!*

Tom dabbed at his eyes again and put his arm around me and gave me a squeeze.

And we sat in silence.

23

July 4. 1973

Miyako called shortly after midnight. Sam's water had broken and her contractions were starting again, coming closer together. Tom and I quickly dressed and ran downstairs to the front entrance of Tom's apartment. Yuji, Tom's driver, was waiting by the open door of the limo.

We sped through the dark streets of Tokyo and on to Yokota. By the time we got to the hospital, Sam had already been moved to the Delivery Room. The nurse in attendance at the door showed me how to scrub down and put on a hospital gown. Then she escorted me into the room. Tom and Miyako stayed in the hallway waiting room

"This is the time for you, the three of you," Tom said.

Sam looked like she was in incredible pain. She was covered with sweat, her hair was matted, and the veins in her neck and on her forehead were popping out as she strained with each contraction. She was taking short, shallow breaths.

The doctor, whom I hadn't met previously, was coaching her.

"Push, push,pushpushpush!"

I felt totally helpless. If I had been with Sam during her pregnancy, I could have taken Lamaze classes with her. But I had been TDY, away from her, for virtually the entire time she was pregnant. The only thing I knew about natural childbirth, other than what I had read in the books at the base library, was the movie they had shown us in Physiology class at the Academy, back in 1965. For a 20-year-old, that movie had been pretty overpowering.

I rushed over to Sam and held her hand. She was now between contractions, taking long, deep breaths.

"Breathe with me," she said, looking into my eyes, "and stop looking so scared!"

I tried to time my breaths with hers, and I started to get lightheaded.

"In through the nose, out through the mouth," she said, "and make your inhalation breaths the same size as your exhalation breaths."

I timed my breaths to match hers, and started feeling better.

"Ice," she said, looking at the cup of ice on the night stand.

I passed the cup to her, and she held a chip of ice in her mouth and handed the cup back to me.

Now the contractions were starting again. Sam took in a deep breath, then started short, shallow breaths again, pushing hard. She was squeezing my hand so tightly I was about to complain, then I thought about the pain she was enduring and felt like a total idiot.

But I was having a hard time keeping up with her breathing.

A nurse came up behind me, put her hands on my shoulders, and guided me to a seat. I didn't want to let go of Sam's hand, but I was feeling faint.

"Just sit down for a minute until you feel better," the nurse said, "She'll be fine without you for a minute."

I felt a short wave of nausea pass over me, and I lost track of time. Finally, my head cleared and I suddenly felt fine. I carefully stood up and went back to the bedside. Sam needed me, and I'd be damned if I was going to let her down.

I stood next to her bed, breathing with her, for the next three hours.

And suddenly, our baby was born.

The doctor looked at me.

"Do you want to cut the cord?"

"Yes," I answered, "but I don't know how to do it."

"I'll show you," he said, "First, we wait until we don't feel a pulse in the cord any more."

I put my fingers on the umbilical cord where the doctor pointed and squeezed gently.

"Okay, I think it's stopped."

"Good. Now we're going to put a clamp here, and here," he said, "and we put this gauze pad right where you're going to cut."

He handed me surgical scissors, and I cut the cord. A little blood saturated the gauze.

"That's all there is to it," he said, "Now, we have to clean up your son a little, and I'll let you hold him."

My son! I had a son!

I heard a faint slap, then I heard an infant crying. And then the doctor handed him to me. His skin was blotchy, he was slimy, and he was crying.

And he was the most beautiful baby I had ever seen, although it was hard to see through my tears, because I was bawling my eyes out.

Sam was spent. She looked exhausted. But she wanted to hold the baby.

"Let me see my Johnny," she said.

I carefully placed the baby next to her in the bed.

"So," the nurse said, "the baby's name will be John?"

"Yes," Sam replied, "John Adams Hancock."

24

July 4, 1973

We were in the recovery room now. Sam was sleeping, and I was resting on a sofa against the wall. I've never seen her look more beautiful.

I got up to visit the nursery, to see my son, and the sound of my stirring woke her.

"Would you like a visit from our newest family member?" I asked.

"Yes. I really need to hold him again to make sure I wasn't dreaming."

I went to the nursery and got the attention of the nurse who was attending to Johnny.

"Can you bring him by my wife's room? She's awake now."

"Right away, sir."

I went back to the room, followed shortly by the nurse carrying our son. She placed Johnny into Sam's arms, and Sam beamed.

"I think we did pretty well," she remarked.

"You did all the heavy lifting," I replied, "but I'm thrilled with the result."

We took turns holding Johnny, and finally I got up the nerve to discuss the name choice.

"You know, of course, that he's going to be getting ribbed about his name for the rest of his life. Every time he needs to sign something, people are going to say, 'Put your John Hancock right here', then they're going to snicker."

"I thought about that, Honey, and I realized what an honor it is to be born on the Fourth of July and have the name John Hancock. Choosing the name John was really a no-brainer. And if he gets a little heat for his name, I'm sure he can handle it. You know, the original John Hancock never shied away from adversity. When he committed treason by signing the Declaration of Independence, he signed his name in bold letters, so that King George would be able to read it without his glasses."

"Fifty-six patriots signed that document," she continued, "and they all pledged their lives, their fortunes, and their sacred honor. So, I think our son will be able to handle a little ribbing from time to time."

"You really do know your American History. So how did you choose the middle name?"

"John Adams was also one of the original signers,

and, like our Johnny's father, he really had guts. He was the only attorney willing to defend the British soldiers who killed the five civilians during the Boston Massacre. He did that in the face of incredible animosity from the civilians. And the Fourth of July is an important date for him, also."

"Right. Because he was one of the signers," I said. I was anxious to show Sam I knew a little American History also.

"Plus, that was the date when he died, fifty years later."

"You're kidding."

"No, truth is sometimes stranger than fiction."

"I guess it is. I can see I'm going to need to learn a little more about our country's history."

"A little more?" she smiled, "I can see you still have your sense of humor."

25

July 16, 1973

I had returned from military leave the previous night, and was actually anxious to get back to the office. My work, other than the day-to-day facilities scheduling, had piled up, and there were several projects with short suspense dates that needed immediate attention.

More important, I was due to be removed from DNIF status, and I was really chomping at the bit to get back into the Phantom. I called the Flight Surgeon's office and made an appointment for a follow-up visit in the afternoon. I had checked in with his office when I had first arrived back at Kadena from CCK, and had informed him that I was really anxious to get off of DNIF. He had been expecting to hear from me.

"Good morning, Captain Hancock. You look like you're feeling a lot better than when I last saw you."

"And I feel great, Doc. I'm ready to get back into the cockpit."

"Okay, let's take a look."

The Flight Surgeon proceeded to give me the most

complete physical I'd had since my Initial Flight physical back at the Academy. In addition to drawing blood and checking my vital signs, he spent a lot of time pressing on the glands under my chin, and feeling my abdomen to assess my internal organs. And at the end of the process, he declared me fit to fly.

"You are officially off DNIF status," he announced, as he signed the form in my medical record folder.

"Thank you, Doc. How do I get the information to the squadron?"

"Here," he said, as he handed me a copy of the form, "give this to the squadron Admin section. We'll follow up by sending a copy to Flight Records Section."

I was pumped. I drove down to the squadron and handed the Flight Surgeon paperwork to Sergeant Molloy.

"I'm back on status, Sarge. Can you arrange for my re-currency flight as an attached pilot?"

I figured I would take the C-130 over to CCK and get on the flying schedule pretty quickly.

"Sorry to tell you this, sir, but you're not on the attached flier list."

"There must be some mistake," I protested, "I just got off DNIF status, and the Wing Staff pilots fly with the squadrons."

"Sir, I'm sorry, but Lieutenant Colonel Milner specifically directed that you are not to be placed on the attached flier list. He said the squadron doesn't have sufficient flying hours to support any more attached pilots."

Milner, that bastard, had done it to me again. I knew it would be fruitless to discuss this with Sergeant Molloy. I left the squadron, seething, and went directly to the DO's office.

"Hi, Amy. Would it be possible to see Colonel Wilson?"

"He's in a meeting right now, Captain. I can set you up with an appointment for," she scanned her daily planning calendar, "1500 today. May I tell him what this is about?"

"It's about my attached flier status. Thank you, Amy, I'll be back at 1500."

I went back to my office to catch up on work until 1500.

It was really hard to concentrate.

26

July 16, 1973

Amy escorted me into Colonel Wilson's office, and I saluted him as I faced his desk. This was different from my usual visits to his office to address routine training matters, and I wanted to set the proper tone.

"Have a seat, Hamilton," he said, as he returned my salute and motioned toward the couch. After I sat down, he joined me there.

"I think I know why you're here, but why don't you fill me in."

"Sir, I just was released from DNIF status, and I'm supposed to be flying with my old squadron as an attached pilot, but I just found out I've been removed from their attached flier list."

I really wanted to tell the Colonel that I knew the reason Milner had kicked me out of the squadron, and now removed me from the list. It was because I hadn't gone whoring with him. But it would seem petty if I said that, and it would be a totally unsubstantiated accusation, he-said versus he-said. Besides, I suspected that Colonel Wilson had an idea what was going on in the squadron.

"I had a talk with the Ops Officer," Colonel Wilson said, "and he said they're just plain out of flying hours. You manage the training program, and you know how thin they're stretched."

"Sir, how can I adequately manage the squadron's training program if I don't have an opportunity to see the operation first-hand? Every other Wing Staff member flies as an attached pilot with one of the squadrons."

I didn't need to point out that Colonel Wilson traveled to CCK – at the controls of an F-4 – to maintain his own F-4 currency. All the other Wing Staff pilots, other than the ROAD Majors, flew the F-4 for currency.

"The Majors at O&T don't fly anything at all."

He was talking about the ROAD Majors.

"Sir, that's because they were originally assigned to Kadena in nonflying staff positions. They've never been qualified in the F-4. But the other Wing personnel, like the Wing Weapons Officer, all fly with the squadron."

"Hamilton, some day you're going to be an Ops Officer or Squadron Commander. In that position, you'll be expected to manage your squadron's resources. And you sure wouldn't want someone from higher up micro-managing your squadron and second-guessing your decisions. If the squadron tells me they don't have available flying hours, I have to take them at face value. I'm really sorry, but flying with the squadron is not in the cards for you."

He got up and retrieved a form letter from his desk.

"Don't worry, Hamilton, you'll still get to fly. Take this form to Major Riner, at Base Ops, and he'll set you up to be an attached pilot with his unit."

I was very familiar with the Base Ops flying operation. I had seen it in operation several years earlier, when I had been flying T-39 Sabreliner jets out of Yokota and had transited Kadena. Unlike our operation at Yokota, Base Ops had an antique T-29, a propeller-driven twin-engine airplane. I had flown in the back of T-29s when I had taken a Navigation course at the Academy. Even back then, in 1966, it was an old airplane. It looked a lot like an airliner from the 1940s. It had a three-person crew, it was loud, it was slow, and it wasn't an F-4.

I took the form the Colonel handed me, saluted, and left his office, doing my best to not display my emotions. I made it to the privacy of my car before I broke down.

27

July 16, 1973

I looked around to see if anyone had observed me in my car. There was no one in the area. I adjusted the rear-view mirror to look at my face to see if anyone would be able to tell that I'd been crying.

As I looked in the mirror, it hit me. What the fuck was so important about flying an F-4 in the peacetime Air Force?

I felt like a complete idiot, and an ungrateful one at that. Less than two weeks ago I'd held my son, my first-born, in my arms when he was less than one minute old. And he was perfect, totally perfect, completely healthy. I had a terrific wife that loved me unconditionally. I'd gotten to fly the top-of-the-line fighter in combat, and had been lucky enough to get 100 missions over North Vietnam before the war was called off. And less than two months ago I'd finally scored aerial victories.

And now, even though I wouldn't be flying a fighter, I'd still be flying.

And then I thought of all my friends who had never

made it home from the war, or who came back with permanent, serious wounds, some visible, some not. Suddenly, I was no longer upset. It was like a giant wave had swept over me and carried away my sorrow, my stress, my angst.

Sure, I could have kept my fighter by going whoring with Milner, but I would have lost much more in the process. If I had gone to the Dirty Dozen, I would have lost my sense of self-respect. I would have sabotaged the relationship Sam and I had, a bond that we always thought was special. And I might have picked up some disease and infected the most important person in my world — actually, now that I was a father, Sam was one of the two most important people in my world.

In the overall scheme of things, flying a fighter wasn't all that important now. I'd had my fun, gotten my rocks off, and now it was time for me to be more than just another jock. It was time for me to be, as they said at the Academy, an officer and a gentleman.

I squared my shoulders, started my car, and drove to Base Ops.

28

July 16, 1973

Major Riner was expecting me, but wasn't expecting to see me smiling.

"Hello, sir. Colonel Wilson said you could use me as an attached pilot, and I'm really looking forward to getting back in the cockpit."

Major Riner looked at me with a mixture of shock and surprise. He probably wasn't sure if I was sincere, or being a wise-ass.

"You're really happy to be flying a T-29?"

"Sir, I just got off two months of DNIF, and I'm happy to be flying anything. And, deep inside, I was hoping I'd get a chance to fly something with round engines before they totally disappear."

"Well, Ham," he said, as he shook my hand, "you're right about that. There aren't many R-2800 Twin Wasp engines in service any more. It's kind of like going back to the early days of aviation." He walked to the office door. "Let me introduce you to the Convair."

I followed him out the back door of Base Ops to

the flight line, and we walked the short distance to the large aircraft that was parked in the VIP reception area. We climbed the portable stairs that were positioned at the left forward entry door and entered the airplane.

Before we entered the cockpit, I looked to my right, toward the back of the airplane, and was really surprised. When I had flown in T-29s at the Academy, the aircraft were configured as a Navigation trainer, with about a dozen Nav stations in the back. This airplane had forty plush passenger seats and powder blue carpeting. This was a real airliner.

"The civilian designation of the T-29 is the Convair 240," Major Riner explained. "It was introduced into airline service right after the war, and was the first pressurized airliner to see service. Let me show you the front office."

When I sat in the cockpit, I felt a true sense of aviation history. The airplane had a feeling, maybe it was a barely perceptible smell, of a workhorse that had seen a lot. The throttle quadrant looked a bit different from what I remembered about propeller airplanes, from my days of flying the O-2. I saw two throttles, and two mixture controls, but no propeller levers.

"Where are the prop levers?" I asked.

"They're back here," Major Riner answered, pointing at the rear of the throttle quadrant. "The Flight Engineer owns these. He adjusts the props, then he tells us what power we can set."

"Oh."

Flight Engineer. That was going to take getting used to. In all of my flying, up until now, I was in charge of the engine controls. Now there would be a Flight Engineer – an Enlisted troop at that – who would tell me what power I could use. Yeah, this would take some adjusting.

"When can I start flying?"

Major Riner seemed pleased that I was anxious to start flying, and not bitching about losing my fighter slot. I suspect he had heard about what had happened to my attached flying status.

"As soon as you pass your closed-book aircraft systems exam," he said, as he reached into a closet in the cockpit and pulled out a T-29 Flight Manual. "Study this Dash One, and let me know when you're ready to go flying. There will be a 100-question exam on aircraft systems, procedures and flight profiles, and then we'll take a local flight. I saw from your records that you were an IP in the T-39, so we'd like to make you an AC as soon as we can."

I liked the idea of becoming an Aircraft Commander quickly.

Every Air Force aircraft had a Flight Manual, and

they were all titled "Technical Order such-and-such-aircraft dash one". The T-29 Flight Manual was officially T.O. 1-T29-1. The Dash One for the T-29 was much thinner than the one for the F-4, but had a lot of procedures that would be new to me.

I flipped through the Dash One and saw a lot of unfamiliar terms and systems. This may be a slow, old airplane, but flying it wasn't going to be a walk in the park.

"Sir, it looks like there's a lot of information in here that will be new to me, but I think I'll be ready for the test, and the flight, next Monday."

"Okay, Hamilton, I'll put you on the schedule for Monday at 1500."

"Thank you, sir."

My graduate studies would have some competition for my attention. I had one week to get ready for the T-29.

29

July 23, 1973

I've been very fortunate to have a near-photographic memory. It's not perfect, but it's pretty good. It served me well at the Academy, and again in Undergraduate Pilot Training. A lot of people mistakenly think that a photographic memory gives someone an unfair advantage in school, in college, and in business. That's not really true.

Taking a test when you have a photographic memory is like taking an open-book exam. Sometimes those are the hardest kinds of test to take. They require understanding and application of the material, not simply rote memorization. So, when it came to advanced courses in college, my memory gave me a minimal edge, if any at all.

But preparing for a closed-book aircraft exam was really a piece of cake. I was able to pretty much memorize every page of the Dash One, even including some terms I didn't fully understand. For example, I knew the procedures that required feathering a propeller, and I knew what it meant to feather a propeller, from my time in the O-2. But I didn't know how an unfeathering motor worked, and I didn't know what an unfeathering accumulator did. But I was ready for the test. And I was sure ready to fly.

I sat down and banged out the test in about fifteen minutes. The multiple-choice questions were taken verbatim out of the Dash One, so it was really easy. I stood up and walked into Major Riner's office with the answer sheet.

"Are you giving up?"

"No, sir, I'm finished."

"So soon?" he asked, incredulously.

"Yes, sir, it was pretty straight-forward."

"I'm tempted to accuse you of looking in the Dash One to answer the questions, but there is no way you could have looked up all the answers that quickly. Let's see how you did."

Major Riner placed a plastic master answer key over my answer sheet and went down the columns of blackened circles. It didn't take long for him to grade my test.

"Well, this is a first for me, Hamilton. You got a perfect score, and you finished the test faster than anyone has ever done it before."

"Well, sir, I'm pretty anxious to get back to flying."

"I should say so! Okay, let's go."

Major Riner opened his bottom desk drawer and grabbed a helmet bag. I could see it contained several aircraft headsets, along with two aircraft checklists with plastic pages. I followed him to an office down the hall, where a Sergeant was sitting at his desk.

"Sergeant Withers," Major Riner said, "I'd like you to meet Captain Hancock."

"Pleased to meet you, sir," Sergeant Withers said, as he stood and shook my hand.

"Sergeant Withers will be our Flight Engineer," Major Riner announced. He turned to Sergeant Withers. "Time to go fly."

"What? I thought we wouldn't be going for another hour."

"Captain Hancock is Speedy Gonzalez when it comes to test-taking. Let's go."

We all walked out to the airplane, which was now located in a different part of the ramp. As Major Riner and I climbed the stairs to the entry door, Sergeant Withers started the preflight inspection.

"The Sarge will take care of the walk-around," Major Riner said.

For most pilots, performing the walk-around

preflight inspection is not fun. But it's the price they have to pay to go fly. Having someone else do it was a nice change.

Major Riner spent a good deal of time showing me around the cockpit. He showed me how to adjust the seat and rudder pedals, where the light switches were, and went over the controls and indicators, which I had already committed to memory. When we got to the landing gear lever, I knew I was *really* in an antique airplane. The gear handle was made of wood!

Major Riner called for our Air Traffic Control clearance and received permission to start engines. By this time, Sergeant Withers had entered the airplane, closed the door, and seated himself in the cockpit. We completed the Before Start checklist and then Major Riner demonstrated how to start the Pratt & Whitney 2000 horsepower R-2800 Twin Wasp engines.

"That's the same engine that's on the F4," he smiled.

I gave him a quizzical look.

"What?" I asked.

"That would be the F4F Wildcat," he continued, "a Navy fighter from World War II."

"Oh." I gave a wan smile.

"So, here's the deal with starting," Major Riner

said. "First, we open the Cowl Flaps and rotate the starter to the number one engine." He pointed at the Starter Selector switch. "Then, we press and hold the Starter button, and watch the engine. We want to count nine propeller blades, then we''ll rotate the Magneto switch to Both and press the Ignition Boost switch." He paused.

"Oh. Okay. So that starts the engine?"

"No. That's when the fun begins. We have the engine rotating, we have the ignition turned on, now it will be time to give it gas. We start by pressing the Prime button, then advance the Mixture, just a little, and feed in some Throttle, based on how the engine is starting. When the engine catches, release the Starter button. If the engine doesn't catch, you may need to tickle the Prime Switch."

"Sounds pretty easy," I said, "if you have hands like a concert pianist."

"You'll get the hang of it pretty quickly. I'll demo the first start, then you'll do the second."

He reached across me to the starter panel and artfully started the engine. He made it look easy. Then it was my turn.

"One last thing you should know," he announced, "If you get a backfire during start you owe Sergeant Withers a case of beer."

I was grateful I had memorized the starting procedure in my studies. I reached down and let my fingers do a dance on the buttons, while guarding the Throttle and Mixture controls. The giant radial engine belched white smoke as it roared to life, but it didn't backfire. The engine had a throaty sound reminiscent of the World War II fighters I used to see at air shows when I was a kid.

After we completed the Before Taxi checklist, we eased the throttles forward and the engines gave their distinctive staccato growl as we carefully moved forward. When we were cleared for takeoff, Sergeant Withers ran the propeller controls to Full Increase and tapped my hands. I smoothly advanced the throttles, with Major Riner guarding my hands, and the engines gave a throaty roar.

And I didn't get a backfire.

30

July 23, 1973

As the T-29 lifted off and climbed out, we retracted our flaps on schedule, adjusted the cowl flaps and trimmed for level flight as we entered the practice area east of the island of Okinawa.

Performing our air work, I realized something I had forgotten a few years earlier – at altitude, the sensation of speed is nonexistent. Going Mach 1 on the deck is an incredible rush, but going Mach 1, or even Mach 2, at altitude has the same feel as flying at 300 knots. Unless you're close to the ground, there is no real visceral feeling of speed.

And I was enjoying flying the T-29. Part of the enjoyment was probably because this two-month layoff was the longest I had ever gone without flying, but another part of it was the allure of flying an antique airplane.

And this was really an antique. The instruments were basic round-dial displays. The T-39 and the F-4 had modern Horizontal Situation Indicators, but this airplane had the same basic instruments as the O-2 I had flown in Vietnam. It even had the precession-prone

J-8 Attitude Indicator like the one in the T-37 basic instrument trainer. My instrument scan came back pretty quickly, probably because of my time in the O-2. I was doing well in the air work maneuvers, and I could tell that Major Riner was pleased.

"Now let's practice engine-out work," he said.

Next thing I knew, he had pulled the Mixture on the number two engine to Cut-off. The airplane yawed, and I dutifully stepped on the left rudder to keep it flying straight. In all honesty, it wasn't as dramatic as I had expected. It was about like an engine failure on a T-39, which has engines much closer to centerline thrust.

"Not too bad, is it?" Major Riner smiled, "That's because of the Auto-Feather system. When we get an engine failure, the Auto-Feather system automatically feathers the prop on the dead engine. You know what it means to feather a prop, don't you?"

"Yes," I said, "We had to feather the prop on the O-2 when an engine failed. But it didn't occur automatically."

Feathering a propeller was a procedure to stop the propeller on a dead engine from spinning – called windmilling – and creating excessive drag. Once a propeller is feathered, the blades align to a streamlined position and stop turning, creating much lower drag.

"As long as Auto-Feather is working, an engine

failure is pretty easy to handle. Now let's see the engine failure without the Auto-Feather system."

He advanced the Mixture and hit the Unfeather button, and the engine started quickly. While he was doing this, the Flight Engineer was managing the Cowl Flaps. Then he turned the Auto-Feather switch to OFF and pulled the left engine Mixture lever to Cut-off.

This time the aircraft yawed violently. I jammed in the right rudder, and could really feel pressure in my right leg. With the propeller not feathered, the dead engine was really creating a massive amount of drag. I could see I would need to get to the base gym and start doing some heavy squats to strengthen my legs.

We practiced engine-out maneuvering, with the engine feathered and unfeathered, and performed other air work, such as slow flight and precision climbs, descents and turns.

"Looks like you have a good handle on the air work. Let's have some fun and enter the pattern."

The landing pattern is where, literally, the rubber meets the road. It's easy to have a good feel for the airplane when you're flying at altitude, but the real test of a pilot's skill is his ability to manage the last several inches of the flight. In most airplanes, the goal of the landing is to alight smoothly onto the runway.

The F-4, my previous airplane, was not like most

airplanes. It was designed to land on aircraft carriers by slamming onto the deck with a force that would instantaneously dissipate energy and airspeed. And that was the way we flew the plane in the Air Force, when there wasn't an aircraft carrier anywhere in sight. But that was the way the airplane was designed, and the way we flew it.

I'll admit there were times, when I was light and landing on a long runway, when I would attempt to grease it on. And I got to be pretty good at it. There were even times when I'd say to my WSO, "Turn up your Aural AOA."

The Aural Angle of Attack was a tone in the helmet headset that indicated the angle of attack. During an approach, when the airplane was on speed, the Aural AOA would emit a solid tone. This tone would immediately stop when the aircraft landed.

One time my WSO asked, "Why should I turn up the Aural AOA?" and I answered, "So we can tell when we've landed." And, on that particular flight, I had a real grease-job. The only way I could tell my wheels were on the runway was when the tone stopped. It wasn't the right way to land the F-4, but it was satisfying as hell.

Now it was time to see if I could grease on the T-29. Although the airplane weighed in at about the same as the F-4, it was a lot bigger. It was 75 feet in length, compared to the F-4's 58 feet, and had a 90-foot wingspan, compared to the 38-foot span on the Phantom. And it had a control-wheel yoke, while the F-4 had a stick.

Unlike the F-4, we would not be performing an overhead pattern, the airport traffic pattern used by fighters because it was an expeditious way to land a lot of airplanes in a brief period of time, like when they're recovering from a combat mission. We were going to fly a wide rectangular traffic pattern, the kind of pattern we fighter jocks derisively called a "bomber pattern". Major Riner demonstrated the first pattern.

And we were really wide! While we were on downwind, I jokingly said, "Should I get us a new altimeter setting for this area?" The regulations require pilots to reset their altimeter settings every 100 miles.

Major Riner smiled.

"Welcome to the world of big iron," he said.

I paid careful attention to his pattern, especially his final approach and the landing attitude. It seemed to me that the airplane sat a bit higher than the F-4, but not really a whole lot more. During the landing flare, the nose was noticeably higher. The tires gave a satisfying chirp as he smoothly landed the plane and performed a touch-and-go.

"Your airplane," he said as we climbed out.

"Roger," I responded, "landing gear up. Request closed pattern."

He called tower and received clearance for a closed traffic pattern. What I really wanted to do was pull up into a tight-as-hell pattern and show him how we fighter pilots do it.

But I wasn't a fighter pilot now, and I wanted to do this the right way.

I gently banked to a wide downwind, called for gear extension as I came abeam the touchdown zone, and called for flap extension on schedule. I turned base to put myself on a 2-mile final, and set up with a stabilized final approach. Throughout this pattern, the Flight Engineer had been adjusting the prop controls and reaching up to fiddle with the mixtures and the cowl flaps. It was a bit disconcerting, but, what the hell, he was doing his job.

My landing was terrible. Just as I was about to flare, the wheels hit the runway, well before I thought we were in a position to land, and we bounced. I executed a go-around and sheepishly flew the next pattern in total silence. Obviously, I needed to recalibrate my eyeballs.

"I think you started to flare a little late," Major Riner commented.

"I think you're a master of understatement," I

answered.

My next several landing got progressively better. First, I flared a bit high, just a little, then I started flaring at the correct height, and my final landings were really pretty good.

All-in-all, I felt pretty good about our flight.

31

August 27, 1973

I was really enjoying the challenge of graduate studies. This was the last day of my first course, and I was apprehensively looking forward to finding out my grade. I had submitted my final project the previous Wednesday, and felt pretty good about it. We had taken our closed-book final exam on Monday, and our final course grade would be a weighted average of our in-class quizzes, our final exam, and our final project.

My final project had been a term paper discussing the use of simulators for aircraft training. I felt that I had performed pretty thorough research, considering the fairly limited resources available at the base library. I had also visited the medical library at the hospital at Futenma Marine Corps Air Station, not far from Kadena, to research the current developments on motion simulation. Since the inner ear is involved in the perception of motion, I cited numerous studies by otolaryngologists and psychologists. All-in-all, I felt pretty confident about my paper. But still, I fretted.

When the class assembled, Jack handed out our graded exams. I received a perfect score. So far, so good. Then he returned our term papers. Most of the papers had grades written on the front. Mine had "See me after class" written on the cover. I wasn't sure what to think. Had I inadvertently failed to properly annotate a quote, perhaps appearing to commit plagiarism?

My stomach churned for the rest of the class. Finally, Jack wished us all well, told us the next class would commence in two weeks, and we were dismissed.

"Hi, Jack. This note says to see you," I ventured.

"Ham, that is the best paper I've ever received. Have you considered submitting it to a peer-reviewed publication?"

My relief must have shown in my face.

"Did I forget to write your grade on the paper? Oh, gosh, I'm sorry! Naturally, you got an A."

"Well, Jack, I wasn't sure what your note was about. This is my first course, so I was a bit apprehensive."

"I sure didn't mean to make you worry. I'm sorry." He paused. "You say this is your first course, and you already told me you are scheduled to return to the States, when, March of 1976?"

"Right. Sometime in the middle of March," I replied.

He looked at the Filo-fax planner in his attaché case.

"It looks to me like you're not going to finish up your Master's Degree before you leave the base unless you double up on courses."

I had suspected as much. The courses ran ten weeks in duration, and there was a two-week hiatus between courses. If I had started taking my course work as soon as I had arrived on base, I would have been able to complete all twelve required courses before my DEROS. But now I would come up one course short if I simply took one course at a time.

"What do you suggest?"

"Well, we offer two courses every term. One course meets Mondays and Wednesdays, the other meets Tuesdays and Thursdays. Now that you've gotten into the swing of things, I think you should take two courses next term, and probably two courses the subsequent term, just to make sure you finish up before you leave. It will be really hard to complete the degree once you leave, since we don't offer these courses anywhere except overseas."

"Thanks, Jack. I'll head over to the Education Office tomorrow and enroll in two courses for the next round."

The next day, I signed up for two courses, and

decided to take two courses at a time until Sam and Johnny arrived at Kadena.

32

September 23, 1973

I had been flying a lot during the previous two months. After four training flights, I had been cleared "solo", which meant I was allowed to fly unsupervised as a Copilot. Most of the missions were flights between Kadena and CCK, carrying troops, mostly enlisted, in support of Commando Domino. We also had some VIP transport missions, which I was comfortable with due to my previous T-39 assignment.

On every other flight the Aircraft Commander and I would trade off flying duties, alternating who got the landing. Most of the missions were one-day out-and-back flights, which allowed me to get into the office every day, so my work didn't pile up too much. I was really starting to enjoy the flying, because I was performing a rewarding mission. On just about every flight, the passengers would come up to the cockpit and tell us what a great flight it was, and they would usually thank us. And, I have to admit, it was kind of fun playing make-believe airline pilot.

After the first month, Major Riner upgraded me to Aircraft Commander. Now I *really* felt like an airline pilot, with a crew of three and carrying up to 40 passengers. I got a kick out of making passenger-address announcements, and I'll admit I tried pretty hard to get that gravelly sound in my voice that I'd heard on flights when I had been an airline passenger. Chances are, the passengers thought it was corny as hell.

The downside of flying a big plane was that it could carry a lot of baggage. And souvenirs. It seemed every General and Colonel in PACAF had a special purchase that needed to be picked up at CCK. And they knew that the T-29 could carry large items.

One time, there was a huge carpet waiting at Base Ops, with a Master Sergeant standing guard over it.

"Sir," he announced, "this carpet is for General Samuels. It cost over $1000, so you need to be careful loading it."

"I'll tell you what, Sarge," I said, "it looks like it weighs a couple hundred pounds. Why don't you find several of your troops to carry it to the plane, and I'll have the Flight Engineer compute the weight-and-balance to see if we can carry it."

I had already done more than my share of go-fer shopping trips for high-ranking officers. More than once I had gone to one of the off-base bicycle shops to purchase a bike, and then had to pedal it back to Base Ops, usually into the wind, and load it onto the plane. It seemed like every Colonel at Kadena thought he could make points with his neighbors by having one of the base T-29 crewmembers pick up something that was cheaper at CCK – and sometimes not by much – than it would cost back in Okinawa. We T-29 crews had become slave labor for the higher-ups. When I had flown T-39s we didn't have that problem, because the airplane was too small to carry any large items.

I had discussed this with Larry, a Major who was also an attached pilot. Larry always refused to do any shopping favors when he flew.

"When I was flying C-130s at Langley," Larry said, "I put my foot down and refused to do any more shopping for people. I had one guy in my church, a former friend, who had seen Noritake china in the BX catalog, and had heard it was cheaper overseas. He cut out the picture from the catalog, with the pattern number, and asked me to pick up a complete dinner set for him. He offered to pay me in advance, but I told him he could pay me afterward, when I found out how much it cost." He paused. "Big mistake."

"I found it at the BX at Ramstein," he continued, "and lugged it all the way back to Langley. It probably weighed fifty pounds, and I had to take it into the VOQ with me at every stop, since I couldn't leave it on the airplane. I shelled out three hundred dollars for that china. Now, here's the incredible part. When I delivered it to him, he said it didn't look like the picture in the catalog. It was ivory instead of white."

I looked at him in shock. "You're shitting me, right?"

"Nope. He didn't want it, and wouldn't reimburse me for it, even though I showed him it was the correct pattern number. Here's the really amazing part – I had declared it with Customs when I came back to the States, and a few days later I received a bill for seventy-five dollars for import duty."

"Wow!" I whistled, "Some friend."

"Former friend," Larry responded.

33

October 3, 1973

The best part about the support flying was that we flew all over the western Pacific area. We flew down to Clark Air Base, in the Philippines, and over to Osan, Kunsan and Taegu Air Bases, in Korea. I'd operated into all of those bases during my T-39 assignment, so I was very comfortable in this environment. Most important, we had a lot of trips to Yokota, and I got to see Sam and Johnny practically every week.

Even though it was usually only a week or so between visits, Johnny looked different, and bigger, every time I saw him. I just couldn't imagine what it would have been like if I had been in the F-4 squadron on permanent TDY.

I had expected T-29 flying to be fairly uneventful. I had been wrong. The one thing I hadn't considered was that I was flying an old, a really old, airplane. Even though maintenance was excellent, being conducted by the Military Airlift Command unit on base, there was no getting around the fact that the airplane was tired. It had been through a lot, and required constant trimming to keep it flying straight. It probably had a lot of bends, buckles and dents in the fuselage that hadn't existed when the aircraft was delivered new. And the engines, the World War II-era engines, were touchy. Very touchy.

I was on a repositioning flight from CCK back to Kadena, with the call sign Spear 29. All of our support flying out of Kadena used the call sign Spear, as in "tip of the spear", signifying Kadena's strategic geographic importance. Suddenly, the number two engine started banging like it was going to shake itself apart any second. Sergeant Withers, the Flight Engineer, was on it immediately, and had the engine secured in a heartbeat. The problem was, the Auto-feather system didn't activate, and we were unable to manually feather the prop. I stuffed in full left rudder, and ran the rudder trim to the stop. The aircraft was in a slight turn to the right, and full left rudder wasn't enough to stop the turn. I banked to the left, and finally was able to control the heading with 15 degrees of bank.

The problem was the incredible drag of the unfeathered right propeller. It was spinning in the slipstream - backwards - and all feathering efforts by the Flight Engineer were unsuccessful. My left leg was shaking from the continuous pressure of full rudder, and I needed a break. I turned to my Copilot, another Captain, Greg Johnson.

"Greg, I need you to spell me on the rudder. Get on the left rudder with me, and hold it as long as you can while I give my leg a rest."

"Got it, boss."

When I was sure Greg had control of the rudder, I eased off and massaged my left leg. I would need to get back on the controls soon enough. First order of business was getting the airplane safely on the ground. We had been flying at 24,000 feet, and were now unable to maintain altitude. We needed to land, and fast.

I've always said I'd rather be lucky than good. Today I was lucky - the weather was severe clear, and we were within sight of Miyako Jima island, which had a 6500-foot runway. I had been navigating by reference to the Miyako VOR, the radio navigation aid, frequency 117.5. Our DME – Distance Measuring Equipment – read 27 miles. There was an airport right in the center of Miyako Jima. A few miles to the west of Miyako Jima Airport, there was another airport, Shimoji Shima. Shimoji had just opened a few months earlier, but it was officially listed as a Private field, and not suitable for our operations. Unless it was an emergency. I could see both airports, and made my decision.

Miyako – my mother-in-law's name. I thought that was a good sign.

I chose Miyako.

I tuned our communication radio to Guard frequency, 243.0.

"Mayday, mayday, mayday. This is Spear 29 on Guard declaring an emergency. We are in a descent to an emergency landing at Miyako Jima."

I received an immediate reply, in a thick Japanese accent.

"Spear 29, this Miyako Jima Tower. You cleared to land, runway 04. Wind 090 at 10, altimeter 29.82 inches."

"Roger. Thank you."

I turned to Greg "I have the airplane."

"Roger, you have the airplane."

I reduced the power on the number one engine, and was able to slightly ease off on the rudder during the descent. I visually set up for a ten-mile final, altitude 3000 feet. That put me on a three-degree visual glide scope. The long final descent meant we would need less power on our good engine, since we wouldn't be maintaining altitude. It was a little easier on my left leg. A little.

I made a good landing and cleared the runway in the direction of the nearby buildings. As I turned off at the intersection, a truck with a "Follow Me" sign met us and guided us to our parking spot. I set the parking brake, shut down the left engine, and breathed a huge sigh of relief.

"Thanks for your help, guys," I said, turning to Greg and the Sergeant Withers.

In return, they told me what a great job I did.

I tried to act modest, but I knew they were correct.

34

October 3, 1973

Back at my original flying squadron, Lieutenant Colonel Milner had DEROSed about two months ago, replaced by a local Lieutenant Colonel, Jim "Robby" Roberts. I had flown on Robby's wing when I'd first arrived at the squadron, and he seemed like a pretty good guy. Then, a week ago, Cocktail Collins DEROSed, and another Lieutenant Colonel had arrived yesterday to take command of the squadron. He was going to be introduced at today's morning Staff Meeting.

When I walked into the Staff Meeting room and saw Scooter Scoville seated at the table, you could have knocked me over with a feather. He had been the Ops Officer of my squadron at DaNang, during my first tour in Vietnam. Even though he was an OV-10 jock and I was in the O-2 section, I had gotten to know him really well. In fact, I had flown in his back seat on the return leg of my champagne flight, after my airplane had been shot up and I'd recovered at an emergency airfield. And now he was a Squadron Commander.

"Hamfist!" he yelled, as soon as he saw me, jumping up from his seat to give me a big hug. "Great to see you!"

"Great to see you, Scooter, I mean, Colonel."

"Are you in my squadron?"

"No, sir. I'm full-time at Wing O&T."

"Which squadron are you attached to for flying?"

"Neither, sir. I'm flying the base T-29."

"I had heard you'd gone to F-4s," he said with a puzzled look.

"I did, sir. I flew my second tour out of Ubon. Then I was assigned as a jock in the squadron you just took over. But when I got transferred from your squadron to O&T, they wouldn't put me on the attached flier list."

"Well, we'll just see about that."

Later that day I received a call from Major Riner.

"Ham, can you come down to Ops? I need to talk to you."

"Sure," I said as I looked at my schedule, "I can be there in about ten minutes."

"Thanks."

I drove the short distance to the T-29 Ops Building, and he was waiting for me.

"What's up, sir?" I asked.

"I just received a request, more like a demand, that you be assigned as an attached pilot to your old fighter squadron."

I didn't know how to respond, but I think my face gave me away.

"I know that's what you've wanted ever since you were assigned to O&T," he continued, "but I sure hate to lose you as an Aircraft Commander. You do a great job for us and, well, we really need you." He paused. "Would you consider becoming dual-qualified, maintaining status in the T-29 in addition to the F-4?"

"Wow! I didn't know anyone is allowed to be dual-qualified," I answered. Back when I was in Undergraduate Pilot Training, a couple of the IPs were dual-qualified in the T-37 and T-38, but it was a rarity. The closest I had ever come to being dual-qualified was flying two models of the F-4 – the F-4D and the F-4E – when I was at Ubon.

"It's within the purview of the Wing Commander. Colonel Wilson said you were specifically requested by the new squadron commander, and the Wing Commander approved it. You won't maintain Combat Ready status in the F-4, but you'll fly attached with them and also fly the T-29 with us, if you're agreeable."

"Absolutely. Thank you, sir."

Because I had been out of the F-4 for less than six

months, the local checkout to regain my currency was brief. I went to the Life Support section, the same section where I had been in charge just a few months earlier, and received my parachute harness, helmet, oxygen mask and survival vest. Then, I received recurrent ejection seat training and took a closed-book aircraft systems exam.

And, the next day, I took a local Qualification check-ride.

After thinking I would never fly the Phantom again, I cherished every flight.

35

October 31, 1973

At 1800 hours, I received a call from Ron.

"Ham, I just received a call from the DO. We need to get to Wing Headquarters ASAP."

"Okay, Ron. I'll be there in about twenty minutes."

"As fast as you can, Ham."

I looked around the BOQ to see what kind of creative outfit I could make. Obviously, this was going to be a no-notice Halloween party, and I felt a little sheepish not having a real costume.

I knocked on a few doors at the BOQ to see if anyone had anything I could borrow. Finally, one of the guys had a dress that he had found in a closet when he moved in. It must have been about a size 16, because it fit me perfectly. I didn't have a long hair wig, so I wrapped a towel around my head, like a woman who had just gotten out of the shower.

I looked in the mirror, and realized what an incredibly ugly woman I would make. But, it was funny. It wasn't all that creative, but it would have to do.

As I drove to Wing Headquarters, I realized how cold my legs felt, wearing a dress. Maybe if I'd had some stockings I wouldn't have been so chilly. Then again, I had hairy legs, which provided some insulation. I realized I had no idea how women put up with it.

I entered Wing Headquarters and ran headfirst into the DO, Colonel Wilson. He was not wearing a costume. He was in his flight suit, and he did not look pleased to see me in a dress. Fortunately, I was not the only one to show up in a costume. About fifteen minutes after I arrived, it was clear that most of the wing staff was in attendance. At least half of them were in some sort of costume.

"Gentlemen," the DO announced, "we've just been notified that the Arabs have embargoed all oil to the United States. Our wing will not be receiving any more fuel for the remainder of the year. We need to get by on the stores we currently have, and we still need to accomplish all of our training. Your task," he looked around the room, making eye contact with each of us, "is to figure out how we're going to do it."

I had been aware of the Yom Kippur Arab-Israeli War that had started a few weeks earlier, but I hadn't realized the dramatic effect it would have on our operation. Now it hit me with full force.

A Major from the Logistics Plans department had somehow come up with a figure, in gallons, of our current fuel supplies. A few of the guys had hand-held calculators. It was amazing what the little devices could do. They could add, subtract, multiply, divide. Amazing. The guys had gotten them at the Pony Store outside the West Gate at Yokota. I decided I needed to visit the Pony Store on my next visit to Yokota.

A Lieutenant Colonel from the Maintenance squadron came up with some fuel figures for operating the F-4.

"Just starting both engines on the F-4, letting the engines stabilize at Idle, and then shutting them down uses 30 gallons."

This was looking grim.

We broke up into working groups, and I teamed up with Bob Miller, a Captain from Logistics Plans, who had a calculator.

I left the group momentarily and went to my office to retrieve the latest training report. Each crewmember had training items, like a specific number of refueling missions or low-level bomb deliveries, he was required to accomplish during the 6-month semiannual training cycle. My report detailed what every pilot and WSO had accomplished so far, and what training events remained.

Bob and I went over every pilot and WSO remaining training event, and calculated how many sorties each crewmember would need to complete his training for the semiannual period. Then we added up all the sorties, and multiplied that number by the number of gallons of JP-4 fuel used on an average mission. We broke the results out by air-to-air missions, which lasted 1.5 hours, and air-to-ground missions, which were 2.8 hours.

It took all night to arrive at a final solution, but we were fairly certain that we could get all of the remaining training accomplished, but just barely. It would require a lot of monitoring of each day's activities, and every pilot would need to maximize his training on every mission.

Although it took a lot of effort to develop the plan, that was the easy part. Implementing the plan was going to be the challenge.

36

November 3, 1973

Colonel Wilson sent me to CCK to make a mass presentation to the fighter squadrons to explain the fuel challenges we would face, and the training plan. He accompanied me. This was my first time getting up in front of a large group of people, and I was understandably nervous. Even though I knew pretty much every jock in the audience, it was still intimidating.

I had prepared some 35-millimeter slides to show our current fuel reserves, typical fuel usage on an air-to-air or air-to-ground sortie, and sample event sets that could reasonably be accomplished on each sortie. When I finished my presentation, I asked if there were any questions. A Major from the back of the room spoke up.

"It sounds to me like you're going to try to micro-manage every sortie we fly. Maybe you're not flying with us enough to realize that it's the Flight Lead who determines what events will be accomplished on every mission."

Before I could answer, Colonel Wilson responded.

"Major," he said, "I think every Aircraft Commander, and every Flight Lead, should be allowed to determine what training to accomplish, *when he owns the airplane and fuel*. But right now, the 18th Tactical Fighter Wing owns the airplanes and the fuel. Like it or not, every one of you are going to be puppets on a string, performing the training we direct, when we direct it, and flying sortie lengths that we direct."

A groan went up from the audience.

"Guys," he continued, "I don't like this a one bit more than you do. But this is the peacetime Air Force now, and our job is to train to be ready to go back to war at any time. And what needs to be accomplished on that training is already established in the regulations. We've been dealt a really shitty hand, and all of us need to pull together to make the best out of a lousy situation."

"So," he leaned forward, resting his elbows on the podium, "let me put it to you this way. You're all adults. We're all on the same team. Perform the training that you, as an Aircraft Commander or Flight Lead, determine you need to do to remain Combat Ready. But log the training we tell you to log, and fly the sortie lengths we tell you to fly."

A cheer arose from the audience.

"And I pity the crewmember who repeats what I just said, outside of this room."

We left the stage to thunderous applause from two hundred jocks.

37

December 17, 1973

Sam and Johnny were going to be arriving soon, and I knew my time would not be as free as it had been up until now. I went back to taking only one course per academic term, since now I was on track to finish up all twelve courses before my DEROS.

I had been periodically checking in with the Base Housing Office to see the status of my application for on-base housing. A week earlier, they advised me that I would be able to accept the keys to an on-base house on this day. I went by to pick up my keys, and also requested some government furniture.

When Sam and I had lived on-base at Yokota, we had accumulated a few items of furniture, but not really very much. A bed, a console stereo, a television, a bookshelf. That was about it. So we would need to borrow living room and dining room furniture, a washer, dryer, another bed, some lamps, plus assorted chairs.

The Sergeant escorted me to the warehouse, and I picked out the items that I thought would meet with Sam's approval. They all looked pretty much alike, so it wasn't too difficult. The Sergeant assured me that everything would be delivered later in the afternoon, and we could return or exchange any items at any time. This was a great example of the way the Air Force took care of its people.

I was really anxious for Sam and Johnny to arrive. I placed an Autovon call to her to let her know we now had a house.

"Honey, we're now, officially, on-base residents."

"That's wonderful, Ham. And in two more days, I will officially be a civilian. Actually, an Air Force dependent."

"Do you feel okay about that?" I asked.

"Absolutely. Before Johnny was born, I was doing something really important, serving my country. I've done that now for four years, and I enjoyed every minute of it. But what I'm going to be doing from this point on is just as important. I'll be supporting you, as you're serving our country, and I'll be raising our son, with your help. And our son is our future. And our country's future."

"Be sure to let me know as soon as you get your travel authorization. Major Riner said he'll make sure we have a *quote* Training Flight *unquote* to Yokota, and we'll be releasing seats to passengers."

"This will be Johnny's first airplane ride, and his father will be at the controls. Very cool."

"I need to run now, to be at the house for the furniture delivery. I'll talk to you tomorrow. I love you, sweet-heart."

"I love you too, Ham. Goodbye."

38

December 25, 1973

A few days earlier I had picked up Sam and Johnny on a T-29 flight to Yokota. Although Sam had been on a flight I'd been operating before, when I was flying T-39s out of Yokota, it was still a thrill for me to get to show her what I did for a living. And I really wanted Johnny's first airplane ride to be with me at the controls.

We got settled into our house, a Capehart model on Christos Avenue, right in the center of the Kadena housing area. Although we had three bedrooms, we both agreed we should keep Johnny's crib in our bedroom, at least until we were completely settled in. We were both adjusting to our new roles as parents and, for Sam, as a dependent.

This was an important anniversary for me. It had been five years since I left for Vietnam, the same day I met Tom, who became my father-in-law. And it had been four years since I returned and proposed to Sam.

Most important, it was our third wedding anniversary. I decided to surprise Sam by taking her to the restaurant that Don had introduced us to several years earlier. I especially liked the name. Sam's by the

Sea.

"With a name like that," I had said to Sam, "how could it *not* be our favorite place?"

Before Johnny was born, all it took to get ready to go out was a quick shower and change of clothes before jumping into the car. Now, it was more like preparing to go on a safari. We had a large leather shoulder bag, which we packed with infant formula, baby food, diapers, wiping paper, bibs, and toys. I could see this would be a big adjustment for both of us.

We had Johnny in his car seat, which was also a baby carrier, and we sat in the comfortable rattan chairs by the big window overlooking Nakagusuku Bay. The view was magnificent.

After we ordered, I looked into Sam's eyes.

"Are you having second thoughts about leaving the Air Force?"

"Not at all," she replied, "As soon as I held Johnny in my arms, I realized this is what I was meant to do."

"Maybe when he's older, when *all* of our children are older," she smiled, "I'll get back into Law, in some degree or other, but my main job, my mission in life right now, is to be the best wife and mother I can be."

"I love you Sam. Happy Anniversary."

"I love you too," she said, as she leaned forward to kiss me, "Happy Anniversary."

39

January 7, 1974

Major Riner ran the Pilots' Annual Instrument Refresher Course. The IRC was a three-day lecture course conducted in the Wing mass briefing room, a theater-like room with about 100 seats. The lectures covered a wide variety of subjects, such as Regulations, Spatial Disorientation, Weather, Instrument Procedures, Publications, and Aerodynamics.

The course culminated with a four-hour 100-question multiple-choice exam. The exam was open book, and required a lot of searching through the dozens of publications each pilot had been issued. The exam questions were developed by the Air Force, and sometimes it would take ten minutes or longer to find a single answer, even if you knew exactly where to look.

Major Riner conducted the course six times a year. Each pilot had a Base Month for his Instrument Check, and could take the exam either one month before, during, or one month after his Base Month. When I saw how worn out Major Riner looked at the end of the third day, I felt really sorry for him. He had been talking virtually non-stop for two and a half days. After the class was over, I approached him.

"Sir, do you need help conducting the course? It looks like a lot of work for just one person."

"I sure do," he responded, "Major Swenson was assisting me up until last month, but he DEROSed, and I'm left holding the bag by myself."

He looked totally worn out, and as soon as I volunteered to help out, he looked like he had just been jolted with electricity.

"I'd be happy to help out, if you like," I said.

"If I like? You bet! Thanks, Ham! Let's take a couple days off, then I'll show you the ropes and make sure you're ready for our next class, in March."

40

March 4, 1974

It was my turn to help Major Riner out with the IRC. He had assigned me one of the easiest classes to teach – Spatial Disorientation, which consisted of showing an Air Force film – and one of the most difficult: Regulations.

There was no way to make the Regulations class interesting. It was dry, boring material that had to be memorized and interpreted. How much rest a pilot is required to have before flight. How many hours of duty time were allowed. What minimum weather was required to commence an instrument approach. When was an Alternate required to be designated. What ceiling and visibility were required for an airport to qualify as an Alternate. The list went on endlessly.

It had looked so easy when Major Riner had presented the material. He had told a few jokes, used stories to illustrate his teaching points, and had kept the audience interested. I, on the other hand, had virtually nothing to say except what was on the briefing slides, which I read as each slide was projected.

When I had practiced my presentation, it had taken

slightly less than 50 minutes. The perfect class length. Now, I was nervous, I had been talking quickly, and found myself on the last slide at the 20-minute point.

"Are there any questions?" I asked, hoping no one would ask anything that would further embarrass and humiliate me.

"Yes," a Captain asked from the back of the room, "Are you going to be teaching any more of the lessons?"

A few muffled chuckles emanated from the audience.

"Okay, you wise-asses," Major Riner said, as he strode onto the stage, "Captain Hancock here has just graciously given you another break before our next lecture. Let's make it 15 minutes."

As the audience got up to stretch their legs, he whispered to me, "Ham, you did just fine. *Illegitemi non carborundum.*"

"Thanks," I said, giving a weak smile. I resolved to do better the next time, and was thankful I had studied Latin in high school. *Don't let the bastards get you down.*

41

March 15, 1974

I received a call from Major Riner. "Ham, I have some news I think you'll like."

"What's that, sir?"

"We're finally going to join the jet age. We're trading in our T-29s for T-39s."

"That's great news, sir."

I had almost 600 hours of T-39 time from my assignment at Yokota. I loved the airplane, and had been an IP in it.

"We want you to be our Initial Cadre IP. They're bringing an airplane down here from Yokota to give you a local checkout. You start flying in a week, and we will get our own birds at the end of the month."

"Excellent. I'm ready to go."

It was bittersweet trading in the T-29 for the T-39. Although I was looking forward to again getting into the Sabreliner, there was a part of me that felt a sense of ennui from losing a piece of our Air Force history. The throaty rumble of the radial engines evoked memories of the World War Two movies I'd seen as a kid. The T-29 was my link to bygone times. It would be sad to see it go. But it was great to get back into the Sabreliner.

The local checkout in the Sabreliner was a piece of cake. Flying the T-39 again was like slipping on a comfortable pair of loafers.

I spent the next several weeks taking our attached pilots on familiarization flights throughout the Pacific, getting them to the point where they would qualify to carry passengers. The guys were amazed at how much quicker the flights to our typical destinations were. We could go to Yokota, Osan, CCK and Clark in about half the time it took in the T-29. And, most important, the plane was small enough that we wouldn't be asked to carry any more souvenirs for the higher-ups.

As I traveled on overnight trips, I tried to get all of my graduate course studying accomplished while I was on the road. Each course required at least ten hours of home study each week, not counting the time in class, and I wanted to have as much time with Sam and Johnny as I could when I was at home. The courses were going well, and I had received a grade of A in every course.

There was great news on the F-4 squadron front. Finally, the jocks would be coming home, at least for a little while. Because of the extreme hardship on the jocks of the 18th Tactical Fighter Wing, PACAF designated an additional F-4 squadron, from Clark Air

Base, to supplement the crews from Kadena.

The two Kadena squadrons would each cycle home for three weeks at a time, while the squadron from Clark filled in. It was a giant weight lifted from the shoulders of the squadron jocks.

Things were starting to look up.

42

March 18, 1974

I had already discovered, from my flying, that a day off from the office wasn't really a day off. Whenever I missed a day at the office, the work just piled up, and I would have more work to accomplish when I got back.

And now, I was going to miss more work. I had been assigned to attend a mandatory three-day Social Actions course. There had been a lot of racial tension in the military during the past several years. It had started with a riot by about 100 black sailors aboard the USS Kitty Hawk, and had spilled over to the other services. The Air Force was looking for ways to smooth things over, and came up with a program called Social Actions.

Social Actions was actually a catch-all for a lot of touchy-feely programs that included race relations, sexual harassment, drug abuse and alcohol de-glamorization. My work was going to pile up at the office while I was going to be subjected to what I considered a different form of harassment.

The course started with a day-long white guilt-in, led by a black Captain who was our instructor. I sat quietly and listened to his diatribe, while he regaled us with all the evils of the white settlers, who first decimated the red man, then enslaved the black man.

Okay, this was payback. If it helped smooth over relations on base, I'd put up with it. But I did take an opportunity to inform the Captain that none of my ancestors had owned any slaves. They had come to America in 1897. Hadn't killed any Indians – sorry, Native Americans – either.

Then it was time to make all of us males feel like shit because we're such sexist slugs. Actually, a lot of the information he presented did seem to make sense. It was fairly common for offices to be decorated with pin-up pictures, and I sensed that it probably made our female members uncomfortable. So, in that regard, it was a good thing to make everyone aware of the effect that their behavior had on others.

In fact, one of the WAF – Women in the Air Force – Sergeants in another office had decided to fight fire with fire. She had posted a photo from Playgirl Magazine on the wall behind her desk, and it made all of us uncomfortable whenever we entered the office. It was difficult to look at the picture and not feel, well, *inadequate*. A few weeks after she posted the Playgirl picture, the Wing Commander issued an edict that all suggestive pictures were forbidden in any office.

On the third day, we spent a lot of time discussing drugs and drug abuse. Frankly, I thought it was a total waste of time. I had never used drugs, wouldn't be able to tell an "upper" from an Advil, and had never even seen marijuana, even in Vietnam.

"And the most abused drug of all," intoned the Captain, "is alcohol."

Great, just great. Next thing you know, they're going to close the bars at the O'Clubs.

He projected a slide on the screen with a list of all the indicators that someone has a drinking problem. If you drink more than five beers a day, you have a drinking problem. If you need a drink first thing in the morning, you have a drinking problem. If you can't wait until you can get to the bar, you have a drinking problem. If you drink alone, you have a drinking problem. If you black out when you drink, you have a drinking problem.

"Wait a minute," I interjected, "I hardly ever drink. But I've blacked out a few times. I know I don't have a drinking problem. I go for weeks, maybe months, between drinks."

"Captain," he leveled a serious gaze at me, "you have a drinking problem. One of these times after you black out, God forbid, you may walk out to your car the next morning and find blood on the front fender."

I didn't know how to answer. So I didn't answer.

After class, I gave three black airmen a lift to their quarters – to prove, I suppose, I'm not a fucking racist – and went home. I needed to run this drinking discussion by Sam, to hear her opinion about my history of blacking out.

I related to her what had transpired in class. She listened patiently.

"Pardon my French, Honey," I said, "but that class was total bullshit."

Sam grabbed both of my hands and looked into my eyes.

"Ham, we need to talk."

43

March 20, 1974

"Honey," Sam said, "I think we need to talk about your drinking. You've told me a lot of stories about how you blacked out when you were drinking in Vietnam, and also when you were at CCK."

I tried to interrupt, but she waved me off.

"I know people came up to you afterwords and told you how much fun you were, you were the life of the party. But you didn't remember any of it, did you?"

"No," I answered sheepishly.

"Honey, that Captain was right. You have a drinking problem. I love you. I don't want to lose you. You're a father now."

"Remember how you used to tell me that joke about the little boy who said he wanted to grow up and be a fighter pilot?" she continued, "And his father told him those two goals were mutually exclusive."

"Yeah," I smiled as I thought back of that joke.

"Honey, it's time for you to grow up. I want you to

stop drinking."

I could see she was serious. And I knew she was right. I squeezed her hands in mine and looked directly into her eyes.

"Sam, I promise you. I will never again have another drink."

And I meant it.

44

May 13, 1975

This past year went by fast. I cycled TDY to CCK six times, three weeks at a time, alternating with the navigators in our office. Naturally, the ROAD Majors didn't go. Each time I was at CCK, I flew a few F-4 sorties for proficiency, usually a mix of practice bombing missions on the range and air intercepts. Even though I wasn't maintaining Combat Ready status, it was great being back in the Phantom.

When I was back at Kadena, I typically flew one two-day or three-day mission each week in the T-39. Usually, I could accomplish some work at the office either before or after the missions, so I didn't get behind on my primary work. Even though I wasn't home every single night, I was never gone for too long. Sam, Johnny and I got into a routine, and life was fairly stable.

We had bought a Kodak Super-8 movie camera at the Base Exchange, and took tons of movies of Johnny. The camera recorded sound along with the movie, and we captured Johnny's first words, along with his first steps. Sam did a great job of recording the important events when I was away.

On this day, for some reason, the DO was not at the morning briefing at 0800. We all sat around the table, waiting. Nobody said anything. We just patiently waited. Finally, at 0830, Colonel Wilson entered the room, looking rushed. We all rose.

"Be seated, gentlemen. I'm sorry I'm late."

He looked at Lieutenant Colonel Scoville.

"Scooter, I need you to pick your four best crews. They're going to deploy in three hours."

"Yes, sir."

Colonel Wilson addressed all of us.

"Gentlemen, yesterday a container ship," he glanced down at his steno pad, "the Mayaguez, was captured by the Khmer Rouge. The Third Mar Div is deploying to Thailand as we speak, aboard MAC C-141s. We'll be providing mission support with four F-4s from Colonel Scoville's squadron and with our T-39."

The Third Mar Div was the short name for the Third Marine Division, based at Camp Courtney, also in Okinawa. They had a proud history. They had been the first combat unit sent to Vietnam, and they were the guys who had protected DaNang when I had been stationed there during my first tour. Altogether, 20 Marines from the Third Mar Div had received the Medal of Honor for their service in Vietnam.

I had celebrated the Marine Corps birthday with them, November 10th, 1969. I got to know some of those guys. If there was any group that could kick Cambodian ass, it was the Third Mar Div.

"We have a lot of work ahead of us," Colonel Wilson continued, "Dismissed."

We stood up as he left, and went back to our offices to get started preparing the wing for combat. When I arrived at my office, there was a note on my desk from Major Riner. I needed to call him back ASAP. I dialed his office and he answered on the first ring.

"Ham," he said, "we have an urgent T-39 mission to Thailand, and I want you to fly it. Sam Johnson will be your copilot. We need to transport six Maintenance troops to U-Tapao in support of the Mayaguez rescue operation."

"How soon do I need to leave?"

"Wheels up in four hours, one hour behind four F-4s from Lieutenant Colonel Scoville's squadron."

"Okay. I'll be at Ops in three hours. Any idea how long I'll be gone?"

"Probably about a week, but it could be longer. You never know."

I put down the telephone receiver and thought back to a conversation I'd had with Major Withers, my

Flight Commander, when I was on my first Vietnam tour, in 1969.

"Let me tell you about what it was like at Kadena a few years ago, flying F-105s. Kadena was a great base, in Okinawa, the poor man's Hawaii. Life was good. We had great flying, mostly weekends off, and all of us married guys had our families there, since it was an accompanied tour."

"Sounds pretty nice."

"It was. Then, one day, out of the blue, we had a no-notice squadron meeting, and we were told we would be leaving for Takhli Air Base, in Thailand, in 12 hours, for an indeterminate time period. Operation Rolling Thunder had just started, and we were going to be part of the initial effort to bomb North Vietnam into submission. I guess you know how that turned out."

I nodded.

"I went from the squadron to my house on base to tell my wife I would be leaving for combat. I walked into our house and she was giving our daughter a bath. As soon as she saw me, standing there in my flight suit, she knew exactly what was happening. She scooped up my daughter from the bathtub, I think she was about three at the time, and said, 'Charlotte, Daddy has to go away for a little while. Give him a kiss goodbye.' And then she helped me pack."

"My wife is a real fighter pilot's wife," he continued. *"She was the squadron commander of our family the whole time I was away. Did everything. Even arranged to have the grass cut."*

I knew I could count on Sam to be that kind of fighter pilot's wife. I went home to pack and tell Sam about my deployment.

She was giving Johnny a bath.

Funny how the more things change, the more they stay the same.

45

May 15, 1975

After I transported the maintenance crews to U-Tapao, I met up with Scooter and his crews. Scooter, Sam Johnson, one of his pilots and I went to dinner at the Officers Club. The WSOs had met up with some classmates from Navigator School, so they didn't join us. The other two F-4 pilots who deployed with Scooter, Joe Josephson and Mongo Monahan, went off base for dinner. They had never been to Thailand, and I suspected they were looking for more than dinner when they went off base.

The next morning, Joe met up with us at breakfast at the O'Club. He looked terrible.

"What happened to you?" Scooter asked, "You look like shit."

"I was up all night barfing my guts out," he answered, "I think I ate something that didn't agree with me."

"Are you okay to fly?"

"Yes sir. I'll be okay as soon as I get hydrated."

"Did Mongo eat at the same place?" Scooter looked really concerned.

"Yes sir."

Scooter went over to the cashier's desk and borrowed their telephone. I saw him dial a number and, after a short time, he hung up, dialed again and spoke to someone. When he returned to our table he looked crestfallen.

"Mongo's in the base hospital. Severe food poisoning."

He looked down at his plate, deep in thought. Then he turned to me.

"Hamfist, I don't want to put pressure on you, but I need your help. Our Wing has been tasked with flying four aircraft in support of this mission. It's important. And now we're short one pilot. Do you think you can fill in for him?"

Does a bear shit in the woods? I tried to suppress a grin. After all, Mongo was sick.

"Yes, sir, I think I can. Although I'm not Combat Ready, I've flown a few range rides recently, and I feel really comfortable in the airplane."

"Okay, then, we need to get you some life support equipment and put you on our flight orders. I've been advised we need to stand bye for further instructions.

We may be flying today, maybe tomorrow. We just need to hang loose."

After breakfast I went to the Life Support Section and tried on Mongo's parachute harness. It wasn't even remotely close to fitting me. Mongo was about six-two, two hundred twenty pounds. The Life Support technician adjusted the harness to fit me, and provided me with a loaner helmet, oxygen mask and CRU-60/P connector. I would need to use Mongo's survival vest.

In the afternoon, we were told to assemble in the base theater. There were a lot of guys there, in flight suits. Obviously, this operation was going to be much larger than just a few F-4s. A Colonel was up on the stage.

"Gentlemen, I'm Colonel Myers, the mission commander. We've had our first casualties of this operation. Yesterday, a CH-53 with 18 Air Police and 5 crewmembers crashed on the way here from NKP."

A map of a section of Cambodia was projected on the screen.

"Just to fill everyone in, two days ago an American-flag container ship was hijacked in international waters by the Khmer Rouge. The crew has been held hostage, and we believe they're being held at Koh Tang Island, here." He pointed at a spot on the map with a yardstick. "The rescue mission will launch at dawn tomorrow. It's predominantly a Navy operation, but we will be providing important support. We will have a mission briefing at Wing Intel at 0400 hours."

After dismissal, Scooter assembled the Kadena contingent in a corner of the O'Club bar.

"Guys," he said, "I want everyone to stay on base tonight. I can't take a chance on anyone getting sick again. We'll meet for dinner here at 1700 hours, then off to the BOQ. We can plan on having breakfast together here at 0230 tomorrow morning."

I was sharing a BOQ room with Sam Johnson, and he wouldn't need to wake up early, since the T-39 was not being tasked for this day's mission. I set my alarm, woke up, and went to the O'Club at 0215. I was finishing up my first cup of coffee when Scooter and the rest of the crew showed up. We ate breakfast pretty much in silence. I was thinking about the guys on the CH-53 who had died two days earlier. It was probably on everyone's mind.

After breakfast, we all walked to Wing Intel, and joined the throng of other jocks in flight suits who had shown up early. Colonel Myers entered the room at exactly 0400. We all snapped to attention.

"At ease, gentlemen. Be seated. We'll start with a time hack. The time is 0401...hack. Major Smith is passing out the attack packages. You will see your line-up cards, along with today's Air Order of Battle. As you can see, the majority of strikes will be conducted by the

Navy with aircraft from the Coral Sea. They will work over the port of Kampong Som and Ream Airfield. The Third Mar Div will be launching an assault on Koh Tang island at sunup."

"Our A-7Ds" he looked toward the SLUF drivers – the SLUF was the abbreviation for Short Little Ugly Fucker, the A-7 – "will be delivering tear gas ordnance onto the Mayaguez, and the Marines in chem gear will board immediately after the delivery. The F-4s from Kadena will support the assault on Koh Tang with Mark-82s and CBU-24s." He looked in our direction. "Nail 23, are you here?" He looked around and identified a young Lieutenant who had raised his hand. "He'll be your FAC over the island. And you've seen the tankers on the ramp on the other side of the field. Their call sign will be Purple Anchor, and they'll be available for any refueling you might need."

"Now," he continued, "Major Green will give the Intel briefing, and Lieutenant Westfall will brief you on the Weather."

We received thorough briefings, although some of the information was spotty. The location of the hostages was still not definitely determined, but the best estimate was Koh Tang Island.

After the briefings, we went to Scooter's BOQ room for a short briefing, then headed out to the flight line.

It was a strange feeling of *deja vu* to be strapping the Phantom back on for a combat mission. Will Winslow, a young Lieutenant, was my WSO. He was excited to be going into combat, and seemed a little nervous. I felt like saying, "Don't worry, kid. I'll take care of you," but thought better of it. It would take performance, not words, to show him I knew my stuff.

We took off just as the sun crested the horizon. I was in the Number Two position, on Scooter's right wing. As we switched to strike frequency, it was apparent there was a lot going on. The Marines had already established a beach-head, and were taking heavy fire from the thick jungle. Nail 23 was already on scene, and gave us a target briefing.

"Spear Flight, your target is an enemy gun emplacement. I anticipate heavy reaction. Target elevation 20 feet, wind calm. We'll start with your Mark -82s. I want you to run in from north to south, with a break to the east. I'll be holding off to the west, over the friendlies. I'm in for the mark."

He rolled in, fired his white phosphorous "willie pete" rocket, and pulled off to the west. White smoke blossomed up through the triple-canopy forest.

"Spear, hit my smoke. You're cleared in hot."

We were in a left wheel over the target, and Scooter was in position and rolled in.

"Lead's in from the north."

Scooter's bombs were right on the smoke. I was next in position to roll in. I put the aircraft into a 135-degree left bank.

"Two's in."

"Roger, two, move your bombs ten meters north of Lead's. That's ten meters short."

"Roger."

As Lead pulled off target, I saw the tell-tale smoke trail of a Rocket Propelled Grenade.

"Lead," I called, "move it around. RPG."

I wanted Scooter to know about the RPG, but my call was pretty much useless. When an RPG is coming up from behind you, there's no way to know which way to break. You might just as likely break into a threat as away from it.

"Stay heads-up to threats," I said to my WSO. I could hear Will's breathing quicken on the hot mike interphone.

I rolled out on my attack heading, and put the gun sight pipper in a position to track up to ten meters short of the smoke from Lead's bombs. I had 8,000 feet to go to my release point. It looked like my pipper would track up to the aim point at the planned release altitude.

"Floaters, two o'clock!" Will yelled.

Floaters are tracers that are stationary in our field of view. I looked to my right two o'clock, and saw a trail of five orange golf balls in trail, getting brighter, but not appearing to move. I watched them for a one-second beat. They were not moving. Not a bit.

Fuck! I needed to get myself on a different delivery trajectory, to fly through a piece of the sky that the tracers would not occupy.

"Hang on, Will."

I pulled hard on the pole to get on a different, steeper flight path. The golf balls moved downward. I pushed over, hard. My head hit the canopy. Thank God for that ballistic helmet. Now I needed to make some mental calculations, and I didn't have a lot of time. I now had 4,000 feet to my original release altitude. But now I was steep. I was no longer in a 45-degree dive. More like 50 degrees. Steep equals long. If I release high, the bombs will hit short. So if I release high just a bit, it will offset the effect of the steeper than normal delivery, which would send the bombs long.

Time for the TLAR bombing system – That Looks About Right. I decided to use my original aim point and release about 400 feet high. Shit! More floaters, this time from the left. Quick jink to the left, toward the golf balls, then hard to the right, to let the pipper track back up to my aim point. Now 1,000 feet to go. RPG launching toward me. Fuck it – big sky.

I reached my adjusted release altitude, pickled off my bombs, pulled to the right, and made a quick roll inverted to see my bombs impact. Right on target. Ah, the beauty of compensating errors! I thought back to my weapons instructor in Fighter Lead-In training.

"Every year, somewhere, a fighter pilot reaches his parameters exactly. The rest of us compensate."

On our third pass, Number Three took a small arms hit, and started pissing fuel out of his left wing. He needed to get back to base, and fast.

"Spear Three," Scooter called, "Pigeons to home plate heading 340. Spear Four, escort Three back to base."

"Three."

"Four."

Now there were just two of us in Spear flight to work over the target.

We made repeated passes with our Mark-82s, and then Nail put us in on another target with our CBUs. We hoped we had done some good for the Marines on the beach, but we just couldn't tell. RNO – Results Not Observed. We couldn't even tell where the RPGs and anti-aircraft artillery were coming from, so we couldn't even kill the guns. They just appeared out of the triple-canopy jungle.

We were winchester – out of ordnance – and made one last orbit over the target while the FAC gave us our Bomb Damage Assessment. We were in the middle of copying BDA, when two RPGs arose from the jungle, both aimed directly at Lead.

Once again, I blurted out, "RPG!" on strike frequency, but it was too late.

Scooter took a hit in his left wing, and was immediately engulfed in flames. Fortunately, he managed to get several miles out to sea before bailing out.

46

May 15, 1975

It was not a sequenced ejection. Scooter's WSO bailed out first, and about ten seconds later the front canopy separated and Scooter ejected. They both had good chutes, and I saw them each deploy their hard-shell seat survival kits and inflate their life rafts as they descended. They did it exactly by the book. Obviously, their Life Support training had paid off.

The WSO popped a smoke as soon as he got into his raft, and a chopper from the Coral Sea was on him almost immediately. I saw a PJ – Pararescue Jumper – lowered into the water to help him get into the horse collar hoist, and they started hauling him into the helicopter.

Scooter had landed about a mile away from his WSO. He appeared to be having a hard time getting into his life raft, and it looked like he may have been injured. Worse, there was a Khmer Rouge swift boat speeding toward him, and it looked like they would get to him before the WSO's rescue was complete.

I was winchester, totally out of air-to-ground ammunition. If I had been in an F-4E I would have had an internal 20-millimeter cannon. But this airplane was an F-4C. A fucking antique. I needed to do something to keep those gomers from getting to Scooter.

I dove down to the water, probably less than 10 feet above the surface, and aimed right for the back of the swift boat. They were firing their .50-caliber machine gun at Scooter, and didn't see me coming from behind them. As I got about 50 feet short of hitting the boat, almost Mach 1, I pulled up and lit my burners, directing the 900-plus degree exhaust right onto the swift boat. I was hoping to get some crispy critters. Instead, all I got was a mighty rocking of the swift boat, but it didn't capsize. I had been going past the boat so fast the heat of the exhaust was too brief. They probably shit their pants, but no crispy critters. The boat kept powering toward Scooter. I needed to do something. Fast.

I pulled up to 7000 feet, swung around and entered a shallow dive, putting my pipper directly on the swift boat. They had swung their guns around and were now firing at me. I could see the muzzle flashes, and heard their rounds hitting my aircraft with a loud metallic clang. I pressed on.

"I'm hitting the Auto-Acq switch, now!" I said to Will, as I put my pipper on the swift boat and selected and armed my AIM-7. The Auto-Acq switch on the left side of the number one throttle allows the front-seater to automatically acquire a target and get a radar lock-on.

"We have a lock," Will replied.

I fired my Sparrow and watched it guide directly into the swift boat. The 80-pound warhead totally vaporized those bastards. The explosion was so powerful I was concerned that the concussion might have injured Scooter, who was only about 100 yards away, but he waved to me as I did a low pass, and the chopper from the Coral Sea gave me call as soon as they picked him up, to tell me he was pretty much okay. He had a broken wrist, but was otherwise none the worse for wear.

When I was sure Scooter and his WSO were safe, I climbed up to altitude and performed a check for battle damage. No leaks, no inoperative systems, no injuries. I RTB'd to U-Tapao, landed without incident, and inspected my bird. There were holes in the leading edge of the right wing, and the leading edge slats were badly mangled, but otherwise no significant damage. Will and I waited for Scooter and his WSO, and after about two hours, they arrived, still damp. The WSO was fine, and Scooter had an elastic wrap on his wrist. We all accompanied him to the Flight Surgeon, and autographed his cast as soon as it dried.

As it turned out, the crew of the Mayaguez had never been on Koh Tang Island, and, in fact, they had already been released. After the tear gas attack on the

Mayaguez, our marines re-took the ship, which had been abandoned. Faulty intel had gotten our jarheads into a pissing contest with the gomers on Koh Tang that resulted in 15 friendly KIA, plus three Marines who were inadvertently left on the beach during the extraction. Reports later filtered back that the gomers had executed them.

We felt like we had done our best, and I felt good about smoking the swift boat. But, with RNO on the BDA, and the unnecessary assault on Koh Tang, it felt like a pyrrhic victory.

47

June 2, 1975

This was an excellent day. Commando Domino officially ended. No more three-week rotations to CCK. The squadron jocks would finally be able to resume some semblance of normal lives. Colonel Wilson called for a flying stand-down, and he addressed everyone in the base theater.

"Gentlemen," he said, "I want to thank you for the terrific job you all did at CCK. You performed your mission with skill and professionalism. I'm proud of all of you."

"Now I have some good news and some bad news." He paused. "The good news is I don't anticipate any more extended TDYs for the foreseeable future, although, as we saw last month, we can never tell when something unforeseen might come up. The bad news is that, now that you're back home, we need to redouble our efforts to get ready for our upcoming ORI."

There was a groan from the audience. An Operational Readiness Inspection is an incredibly thorough evaluation of every mission the Wing is tasked to perform, and the performance specifications are extremely strict. Our F-4 crews would be required to perform operational missions in each of the three DOCs, and, in addition, would take written evaluations in ten different subject areas.

They would be tested on Air Defenses, Weapons Effects, Nuclear Weapons Delivery, No-Lone Zone Procedures, Permissive Action Link Enabling, Aircraft Systems, Air Intercept Procedures, and a host of other subjects. And the three tests that related to nuclear weapons — Nuclear Weapons Delivery, No-Lone Zone Procedures and PAL Enabling — had a minimum passing score of 100 percent. If *everyone* in the Wing did not turn in a perfect test, the Wing would fail the ORI. Talk about pressure!

48

September 22, 1975

The ORI team arrived with virtually no notice. It was intended to be a totally no-notice arrival, but our Command Post had been monitoring all inbound flight plans for several weeks, and saw a C-135 with an unusual call sign headed to Kadena. They alerted the DO, and we basically had about 12 hours of advance notice.

When an ORI team arrives, things happen quickly. The jocks are all recalled to the squadron, and the team evaluates how long it takes for all the squadron members to report. The jocks have been instructed to bring their mobility bags with them for inspection. The mobility bag is a large A-4 bag that has been pre-packed with all items that would be required for a short-notice deployment. Uniforms, flight suits, poopy-suits, everything. If a squadron needs to deploy on short notice, the packing has already been accomplished.

As soon as the jocks arrive at the squadron, they start their closed-book testing. Naturally, there is a member of the ORI evaluation team in the room at all times to monitor the test. Once each test commences, no one is allowed to leave the testing room for any reason, but there is a short break between each of the ten written exams, so the guys can use the latrine, get a cup of coffee, or wolf down a quick meal. The testing lasts pretty much all day.

Once the testing is completed, the war starts.

The ORI team provides the DO with the Frag Order – the designation of targets, run-in courses and Time Over Target – and the DO tasks each squadron with accomplishing the mission. The Squadron Commander is responsible for assigning crews to missions, and he has to provide the flight lineup to the ORI team. Every crew in the squadron must fly a mission. That way, the Squadron Commander can't "stack the deck" by only allowing the best crews to fly.

An ORI team member is positioned at the bombing range at all times, to ensure that the Range Control Officer provides accurate bombing results. Simulated anti-aircraft gun emplacements are situated around the target area, and Surface-to-Air sites are strategically positioned along ingress routes. If a strike flight doesn't avoid these simulated threats, their bombs won't count, since the strike aircraft will be assumed to have been shot down.

The strike flights must also deal with aerial threats in the form of "aggressor" aircraft that can attack at any time, from any direction. In this case, the Japan Air Self-Defense Force F-104s from Naha Air Base are assigned aggressor duty. All aircraft, ours and theirs, are configured with simulated missiles that would record if and when the missiles were fired, and predicted success or failure.

All of us in the DO Wing Staff assembled in the Emergency Mobility Facility, called the "War Room". There was a lot to do, and not enough time to do everything. Our Ops Plans Division had attack templates that could be used on short notice, and we all got to work planning the strikes. Even the ROAD Majors got involved.

This was an around-the-clock operation, and it lasted for five days. As time wore on, we were exhausted. We worked in 12-hour shifts, and the DO was there pretty much full-time, only disappearing for a short time every few hours to eat or to take a quick nap.

This was as close to real combat operations as it could get. By noon the first day, our well-choreographed plans had started to fall apart. I saw, first-hand, the reality of the expression, "No battle plan survives contact with the enemy."

Maintenance had done a great job getting airplanes to crews on time, but still, there were problems. Aircraft 669 had a bird strike shortly after takeoff and had to air abort. Aircraft 442 developed a hydraulic leak as it was taxiing out to the Quick-Check area and had to ground abort. The radar on aircraft 555 didn't pass the BIT check, the Built-In Test that was performed during preflight. It had been scheduled for an air-to-air mission, and the Maintenance crews traded it out with aircraft 778, which would be a strike mission. We kept our fingers crossed that aircraft 555 wouldn't encounter any aggressors, since the radar missiles wouldn't work.

If I hadn't been so busy in the War Room, I probably would have felt like a real outsider. But I didn't have time for introspection or self-pity. I had a telephone up to my ear virtually nonstop for 12 hours every day, coordinating with the squadrons, Maintenance, Logistics and Plans. I was tracking every sortie, assembling reports for the DO, briefing the DO on every mission as soon as I had their results from the range, and trying to keep track of every jock in both squadrons to coordinate with the squadron schedulers.

By the end of the week, we were all like the walking dead. With a 12-hour shift, I was only home long enough to grab a quick snack and a short nap. Sam had made me breakfast, lunch and dinner to take with me, so I didn't starve. I felt totally drained, I had a constant ringing in my ears, and my eyes were bloodshot. The DO looked even worse than I felt.

On the fifth day, we all assembled in the base theater to hear our results. The ORI Team Chief, a Colonel, conducted the briefing, which was accompanied by 35-millimeter slides projected on the large screen.

"Gentlemen," he started, "this is going to be one of the shortest out-briefs I have ever conducted. I'm going to show you some photos we took during the week, and some charts and statistics. But let me cut to the chase right now. Your evaluation is..." he paused for effect, "Outstanding!"

Even though we had been instructed to remain silent until the out-briefing was completed, a huge cheer erupted from the audience.

I looked around at the guys in the theater. They had all done a magnificent job. The crews had gotten their bombs on target, no one had been shot down, we had a successful completion rate, and everyone had an incredible feeling of satisfaction. Even though I hadn't turned a wheel the whole time, I felt really great about my role in the success.

And suddenly, I didn't feel tired any more.

49

September 29, 1975

A week after the ORI was completed, I started working on a project with important and long-lasting consequences. Up until now, there were two fighter squadrons in the 18th Tactical Fighter Wing. They were fairly equally matched in rank, experience and DEROS. Basically, with a three-year assignment, one thirty-sixth of the squadron – two or three guys – DEROSed each month.

The squadron experience levels were not precisely the same, since one of the squadrons – not Scooter's squadron, the other one – had a classified mission in addition to the other DOCs. The mission required special training, so that squadron had, on average, more experienced crews. The squadron had a small number of specially-trained crews, and the rest of their jocks were standard-issue F-4 crews.

One of my jobs at Wing O&T was to determine the squadron assignment for every new arrival, both pilots and WSOs. If a pilot or WSO had been trained in the special mission, he naturally went to the designated squadron. When a pilot or WSO arrived, I would look at his rank, fighter time, flight lead and IP status and

DEROS and would assign him to one squadron or the other, to keep experience levels, rank and DEROS as equal as possible.

Now, with the draw-down of the Vietnam war, the fighter squadrons based in Thailand were being relocated. One of the squadrons, the 12th Tactical Fighter Squadron, was going to be reassigned to the 18th TFW. This made sense, since the 12th had originally been part of the the Wing at Kadena before their deployment to Korat Air Base, in Thailand, in 1970. Back then they had been flying F-105s. Basically, the 12th Tactical Fighter Squadron was finally coming back home.

But there was a problem. We couldn't simply move the 12th back to Kadena as a fully-formed squadron. Since assignments in Thailand were 12-month tours, everyone in the 12th squadron was due to rotate back to the States in 12 months or less. And, in fact, the guys in the 12th with less than three months until their DEROS had already been sent Stateside. So the guys who would be arriving from Korat would all have nine months or less until their DEROS. If we simply stapled the 12th squadron into the 18th Tactical Fighter Wing, we would have massive squadron turnover during the next year. Then, with thirty-six month tours, the Wing would have the same problem three years later.

No, we had to totally reshuffle the deck. And that was going to be my job.

Ron approached me a week after the ORI.

"Ham, we have an important project, really important, and Colonel Wilson told me you're the only one he trusts to do it."

"I'm flattered, sir. What is it?"

"We need to rearrange the manning in all the squadrons to keep experience levels and DEROS dates homogeneous when the 12th is integrated into the Wing."

I could instantly see how big this was going to be.

"This sounds like a really big project."

"Well, you're the one with the Master's Degree. This should be right up your alley."

Actually, it was precisely the kind of project a Master of Science Degree in Systems Management had prepared me for, and I was looking forward to the challenge. I didn't bother to tell Ron I wouldn't officially have my Master's Degree for another three weeks.

I started by gathering data on every jock in each squadron. The Admin Officer in each squadron was able to give me an "alpha roster" listing every pilot and WSO, along with his rank and DEROS. Then I went to the squadron Scheduling Officers and determined which pilots were Flight Leads and IPs. Also, in the special mission squadron, I noted which crews were special mission-qualified. Finally, I went to the Flight Records Section and got the total flying time and fighter time for every jock.

Now I had to get the same information about the 80-plus guys who were going to be arriving from Korat.

I ended up with reams of paper scattered all over my desk, trying to make the pieces fit into this gigantic puzzle.

Complicating this process was the camaraderie inherent in each squadron. Squadrons become like families. There's friendly rivalry between squadrons. The guys, and their wives, form attachments to the other people in the squadron, and it becomes a real challenge to break those bonds.

I stopped by Scooter's office to chat with him.

"Sir, do you have a few minutes to talk?"

"Sure, Hamfist. Have a seat."

We both sat down in the overstuffed chairs against the wall in his office.

"I've been working on the project to integrate the 12th into the Wing, it's been designated Project Smoothflow. Well, I'm going to need to relocate a lot of guys from one squadron to another, basically like shuffling a deck of cards. And guys are coming up to me right and left saying they don't want to be reassigned to another squadron."

"It's funny how that works, isn't it? When we were at DaNang, we were reassigned to different squadrons after 12 months, and it was no big deal. But when we get to a squadron with a thirty-six month tour, especially when there are wives and kids involved, it gets complicated. There's a group dynamic going on, and a degree of intimacy, that's more pronounced in an accompanied overseas assignment than in a Stateside assignment. I'd be willing to bet that every wife in my squadron knows when every other wife is on her period."

"When I was at Air War College," he continued, "we had a lecture by a Psychology researcher about group dynamics. He told us about an experiment with monkeys. Basically, the experimenter put five monkeys in a cage, and there was a banana hanging from the top of the cage, and a ladder. After a while, one of the monkeys figures out how to use the ladder to get to the banana. As soon as he climbs the ladder to get the banana, the other monkeys are sprayed with cold water. After a couple of cycles of this spraying, the monkeys would beat the shit out of any monkey that tried to climb the ladder."

"Makes sense," I said.

"But here's the really interesting part. The experimenter replaced one of the monkeys, and as soon as the newcomer tried to climb up and get the banana, the other monkeys attacked him, and he quickly learned not to do that. Then they replaced another monkey, and another. Soon they had nothing but new monkeys. None of them had ever been sprayed. But they all knew you sure as shit didn't want to climb that ladder."

He paused and withdrew a pack of Camels from the pocket on his flight suit sleeve. He offered the pack to me, I shook my head, and he withdrew a cigarette and lit up.

"Squadrons have their own personalities," he said, "even when everyone in the entire squadron has changed, the squadron personality stays the same. That's what makes it so challenging to effect a culture change in a squadron when there's a problem. You'll find that out," he smiled, "when you're a squadron commander."

"Every time you need to take a guy out of one of the squadrons to reassign him," he continued, "you're going to be on his shit list, no getting around it. His family's shit list also. But you have broad shoulders. You can handle it."

I left Scooter's office with the realization that this wasn't going to be pleasant, but I had a job to do. I would try to accommodate individual requests, but if I couldn't keep a guy in a squadron because he was needed in a different squadron, so be it. I wasn't in a popularity contest.

I had all the information I needed to allocate the jocks to the squadrons, with a good balance of rank for both the pilots and WSOs, fighter time, and retainability. I just needed to figure out how to develop a process to start the shuffle.

Sam saw me staring at the lists of names I had scattered on the dinner table.

"What's the problem, Honey?"

"I have this mass of information, but I'm having a hard time figuring out how to assign the inbound crews and try to keep as many jocks in their original squadrons as I can."

"I think we should play cards," she smiled, as she opened her desk drawer.

"What?"

She took out several packs of 3-by-5 index cards, and placed one card on the table.

"Give me the information for the first guy on your list. Name, rank, position, DEROS, experience, the works."

As I read the information for the first name on my alpha roster, Major Ron Alford, Sam dutifully wrote all the information on the card. We spent the next two hours making up a card for everyone in all three squadrons. Actually, the whole process took about three hours, since I had to make several trips to the Base Exchange to buy more index cards.

"Okay, now what?"

"First," she said, "we'll put the cards into three stacks, representing the squadrons they're currently in."

We went through the cards, and ended up with three stacks, ranging in height from 80 to 100 cards.

"Okay, now we'll separate the pilots in each squadron from the WSOs."

We made more piles. Then Sam went into the kitchen and came back with several colored marker pens from Johnny's toy box.

"Now comes the fun part. We'll let the upper right corner represent rank. A Lieutenant will be red," she started coloring a red triangle in the upper right corner of Beans Beaner's card, "and a Captain will be blue, a Major will be gold, and a Lieutenant Colonel will be silver."

We got busy coloring the corners of the cards to represent rank, fighter experience Flight Lead and IP status, and combat experience. We divided the edges of the cards into sections to represent DEROS, with each edge representing a year, from 1976 to 1979. At some point, Johnny woke up from his nap, and we gave him some blank index cards and let him do some coloring also. He felt like he was helping us.

When we finished, I put a rubber band around the three stacks of index cards and put them on my desk, next to my car keys.

"Honey," I said, "I never would have thought of this without you. I'll be spending the next week or so shuffling through the stacks until I get the balance I'm looking for. Thank you."

"You're welcome. Now let's put Johnny back to bed, and let's see if you can figure out a better way to thank me."

50

December 15, 1975

It took longer than a week to get the cards arranged the way I wanted. A lot longer. I rearranged cards from one deck to another, looking at the colored corners, until I could see, at a glance, that I had arranged them the way I wanted. Finally I had tentative alpha rosters for all three squadrons. I painstakingly calculated the statistics for each resultant squadron, making sure they all had an equal number of DEROSes each month, equal rank distributions, equal Flight Leads and IPs, and equal experience.

One of my graduate courses had been Statistics, and I used my new knowledge to compute the mean and median flight time and fighter time for each squadron, as well as the Standard Deviation. I knew that, sooner or later, someone was going to ask me to explain my results, so I made up charts showing all the information I had amassed. Lots of charts. I showed them to Ron.

"That's great," he said, "and I'm really glad you made up these charts, because General McKenzie is coming here from PACAF. I want you to be the one to give him the briefing on Smoothflow."

I had become fairly comfortable giving presentations, from my experience in Instrument School, but hadn't ever given a briefing to a General, especially the Commander of the Pacific Air Forces. I guess my apprehension showed in my face.

"Don't worry, Ham. You'll do fine. Think of it this way: there's no one on earth who knows more about this than you."

He looked at my charts again.

"You know, Ham, you're a damn fine staff officer. But you're a really lousy artist. These charts look like shit. We don't want to show these to a General. We'll let the Wing Graphics Department make up some really snazzy looking slides."

I made photocopies of my charts, and sent the originals to the Graphics Department with a rush order.

When General "Mac" McKenzie arrived a few days later, I was ready for the briefing. I had practiced it several times, had my timing for each slide worked out, and had gotten a fresh haircut. My class-A uniform was freshly cleaned and pressed, and my shoes could have passed inspection at the Academy.

We assembled in the Wing Briefing Room, and, after introductions, I was called to the podium.

The briefing went well, really well. At one point, as

I was about to switch from a very busy slide, the General interjected.

"Just a second, Captain. It looks to me, from the last line of your chart, that the squadron on column three, line 34, has higher experience levels than the other two squadrons."

There must have been over a hundred numbers on that chart, and the General caught that! I thought back to when I was a Second Lieutenant, at Laughlin, when my T-38 IP, Captain Rogers, had been telling me about his time as a General's Aide.

"Generals don't miss a thing," he had said, "They don't make General if they're not incredibly sharp. Some of them may be assholes, but they're all sharp as a tack."

Now it was time for me to address the General's concern. I had been prepared, and advanced to my next slide.

"General, you can see from this slide that the reason for the difference in Standard Deviation for that squadron is due to the higher experience level required to attend special mission training. We have adjusted for that by assigning more experienced pilots to the other squadrons."

He smiled.

At the end of the briefing, the General looked over at my Wing Commander.

"Excellent project, excellent briefing. I wish all of my Captains could perform like Captain Hancock."

And then it was over. We all stood at attention as General McKenzie left. Afterward, I saw Colonel Wilson talking with Ron. Then Ron came over to me.

"You know, Ham, it looks like you have a really good shot at Major below-the-zone. General McKenzie wants to endorse your OER."

Having a four-star endorsement on an Officer Effectiveness Report is a great first step toward being promoted to Major early, below-the-zone. I had all the other squares filled: two combat tours, all of my PME, great OERs, and a Master's Degree with a perfect 4.0 grade point average. And now a great OER endorsement!

It looked like my career was really on track.

51

February 9, 1976

I had been enjoying the mission of the support flying and attached flying I had been doing for the past two-plus years, but I still secretly harbored a desire to get back into a fighter on a full-time basis. But after seeing the hoops the peacetime jocks had to jump through during the ORI, I was starting to have second thoughts. Flying the F-4 was a real kick, but I wasn't sure I wanted to pay the price of doing it as a full-time squadron jock. In some respects, I suppose I was like the musician who wanted to play in Carnegie Hall, but wasn't willing to practice his instrument.

But I did have what I considered a brilliant idea. I now had a fairly significant amount of IP time, and also had over the magic 500 hours of F-4 time, so theoretically it would be possible for me to get an assignment as an F-4 Instructor Pilot in one of the Replacement Training Units back in the States. The RTUs were where pilots went to become qualified in a new aircraft, and the IPs took them through every phase of training, just as Speedbrake had taken me through my training when I had attended the RTU at Homestead Air Force Base, back in 1971.

The really great thing about RTU duty was the lifestyle. There would be no ORIs, no deployments, no mandatory cross-country flights, and no weekend flying. It would be a very cool way to fly the F-4, especially for someone who wanted to be home every night. In other words, it would be perfect for me.

The drawback, of course, was that as an IP I wouldn't be doing a whole lot of stick-and-rudder flying, I'd be riding in the back seat, instructing. It was no secret that IPs got very little stick time, maybe one or two flights in the front seat every month. But, still, I enjoyed instructing, I was good at it, and I would get back into the Phantom on a full-time basis.

So, getting an IP slot at an RTU became my goal. I didn't even have a preference for which RTU I wanted for an assignment. It could be Homestead Air Force Base, in Florida, McDill Air Force Base, also in Florida, or Luke Air Force Base, in Arizona. I'd be happy with any one of those.

Naturally, I discussed the idea with Sam, and she was more than receptive to the idea.

"Ham," she said excitedly, "it would be so great if you were home every night. And you'll be flying the F-4 full-time. I think it's a great idea."

So, we were sold on the idea. Now it was time to get the Air Force sold also. I made an appointment to see Colonel McNeil, the new DO. Colonel Wilson had

DEROSed at the end of December, and Colonel McNeil had just arrived. As I was planning what I wanted to say to him, I felt like an idiot for not starting this process sooner, while Colonel Wilson was still on base. He had seen me in operation for almost three years, and would have really gone to bat for me. As far as Colonel McNeil was concerned, I was just one of the staff officers he was in the process of getting to know, and his support might be a lot less enthusiastic than Colonel Wilson's. I entered his office with trepidation.

"Captain Hancock reporting, sir," I said, as I saluted.

Colonel McNeil returned my salute and motioned for me to sit on the couch, where he joined me.

"What can I help you with, Ham?"

This was a good sign. He knew my name, and he wanted to help me.

"Sir, I'm due to rotate back to the States soon, and I requested an F-4 RTU IP assignment on my Form 90. I was hoping you could assist me in the assignment process."

The Form 90, also called the "Dream Sheet", was the Air Force Assignment Preference Form, the vehicle used to tell the Air Force your assignment requests. Although there were spaces on the form for three assignments, I only entered one: F-4 Instructor Pilot.

"Ham, I know you've been doing a great job here in O&T, and I'd like to help you. But I think you should know that Tactical Air Command won't assign anyone to IP duty unless he's Combat Ready. As an Attached Pilot you only maintain Basic Qual status."

Basic Qualification status meant simply flying for proficiency, without maintaining any degree of weapons qualification, such as the tasks the jocks performed on the ORI.

"Sir, I think I could get Combat Ready in a heartbeat. I may only have 500 hours in the F-4, but it was all combat. I ended up with 100 missions over the North," I said proudly, "and it all came back pretty quickly when I was attacking Koh Tang," I added.

Colonel McNeil looked shocked.

"How could I have not known this? I assumed you were assigned here as a staff officer without any operational F-4 experience, and that's why you've been flying attached. And I never heard anything about your participation in the Mayaguez rescue. So much for assuming. How come you're not in one of the squadrons?"

Lieutenant Colonel Milner had already rotated back to the States, and I had nothing to lose now by being honest.

"Sir, it's a long story, but basically Lieutenant

Colonel Milner took a disliking to me and kicked me out of the squadron because I wouldn't accompany him to the whorehouses in CCK. He pretty much ran the squadron because Cocktail Collins was never around. After he sent me to O&T, he refused to allow me to fly as an attached pilot. It was only after Lieutenant Colonel Scoville took over the squadron that I was allowed to fly as an attached F-4 pilot."

The Colonel let out a whistle.

"Milner. That son of a bitch. We were deployed to Libya together a long time ago, in F-100s, when he was a Lieutenant and I was a Captain. He was the same way then." He paused, deep in thought.

"When was the last time you were Combat Ready?"

"March 15th, 1973, my champagne flight at Ubon," I answered. I didn't need to check my flight records. The date was seared into my memory.

Colonel McNeil rose from the couch, picked up his phone, and dialed a number from memory.

"This is Colonel McNeil. I need to speak to Colonel Scoville."

Actually, Scooter was a Lieutenant Colonel, which was sometimes referred to as a "telephone Colonel," since it was easier to simply say "Colonel" when asking for a Lieutenant Colonel on the phone.

"Hi Scooter, it's Ryan. I'd like you to check something out for me." He paused, listening. "What's it going to take to get Captain Hancock up to Combat Ready status?" He paused again. "Okay, thanks."

He hung up the phone and returned to the couch.

"Ham, I'll be honest with you. I don't know what the answer is right now, but I'm going to find out. It really pisses me off that Milner…" He was interrupted by the phone. He sprang up and got it on the second ring.

"McNeil." He retrieved a pen and started taking notes on his steno pad. "Okay, Scooter. Thanks for the quick work. Goodbye."

He walked back to the couch, staring at the notes he had just taken. He put the pad down and started counting on his fingers, as though he was searching for some way to make the numbers work out.

"When is your DEROS?"

"The middle of next month. March 17th."

"Shit!" he muttered, looking at his notes, "shit, shit shit."

He turned to face me squarely.

"Ham, I'm not saying this is going to be hopeless, but it's going to be tough. You don't have enough time left here to get Combat Ready. It normally takes two months, and the closest they could shave it is six weeks. There's just not enough time. I'm going to make some calls to MPC and see if they can waive the Combat Ready requirement. I should know something in a day or two."

"Thank you very much, sir. I really appreciate your help."

52

January 13, 1976

I had been fidgeting all weekend, waiting to see if Colonel McNeil had received any information. Then, on Monday, there was still no word. I didn't want to be a bother to Colonel McNeil, but I resolved to pay him a visit if I didn't hear anything by Close of Business on this day. I didn't need to wait until Close of Business.

At 0930 Amy called me in my office and said that the DO wanted to see me. I anxiously entered his office.

"Have a seat, Ham," he said, gesturing toward the couch. He seated himself on the opposite armrest and faced me.

"Ham, I talked to General Briggs at MPC," he began. "I've known him for a long time. We flew in the same squadron when we were both Captains during Rolling Thunder in 1965. One of us," he gave a wry smile, "seemed to do pretty well in his career."

"He personally looked at your file. You have a very impressive record. You're going to have a successful career. A very successful career. But…" he paused, "you don't have the prerequisites to be an RTU Instructor in the F-4. Now that the war is over, the RTUs are flooded with Combat Ready jocks with 1000-plus hours in the F-4. Even with your Air Force Cross, there was no way he could get you that assignment."

The Colonel looked as dejected as I felt.

"The best he could do," he continued, "was to get you an assignment as an RTU instructor in the O-2, at Patrick Air Force Base."

I was speechless. This would be the second time in my career that I'd lost a fighter assignment and ended up flying the O-2. Flying the O-2 in combat was one thing, instructing in it during peacetime was going to be totally different.

Then again, it would be RTU duty, which would provide the lifestyle and stability I wanted. And Patrick Air Force Base, on the east coast of central Florida, was reportedly a great assignment.

I immediately thought back to a conversation I'd had with Beans Beansley, a Lieutenant on his first flying tour of duty in one of the F-4 squadrons. He had just received a follow-on assignment as an O-2 pilot and was really disappointed. When he'd found out I had flown O-2s, he sought me out to get information.

"Oh, you're going to love it," I had told him. "There's probably no job in the Air Force where a Lieutenant has so much responsibility. It's a great career-broadening opportunity."

So, when it happened to Beans, it was career-broadening. When it was happening to me, all I could think was that I was, once again, being fucked.

"Sir," I said to Colonel McNeil, "I really appreciate your taking the time to help me. I'll be honest, I put in my time flying the O-2 already, and I'd had my heart set on an F-4 RTU assignment. But I can promise you I'll do my best at Patrick. And once again, thank you for making the calls."

"You're welcome. I know you'll do great at Patrick, Ham."

"Thank you, sir."

I gave a wan smile and left the office.

53

January 13, 1976

I went back to my office and mindlessly shuffled through the papers on my desk. All of the projects could wait. I needed to get away from the office and get some fresh air. And I needed to talk to Sam.

I drove the short distance to our on-base house, and went in through the kitchen door. Sam was sitting at the kitchen table with Nancy, Larry's wife. They stopped their conversation in mid-sentence when I entered. Johnny was sitting in a corner, playing with some alphabet blocks. When he saw me he quickly rose, ran up to me, and wrapped his arms around my leg.

"Daddy," he smiled. I picked him up, gave him a kiss on his cheek and tousled his hair.

"Ham," Sam said, "is everything okay? What are you doing home so early?"

"Oh, I thought it would be nice to have lunch at home today," I replied.

Nancy knew how to take a hint.

"Sam, I need to be getting back to my laundry,"

Nancy said, "I'll see you later. Nice seeing you, Ham."

"Bye bye," Sam said. As the door closed behind Nancy, Sam looked at me.

"Honey, it's not even ten o'clock yet. It's nowhere near lunch time. What's going on?"

"I just got my assignment," I sighed, "and I don't know if it's a good deal or a bad one."

54

March 15, 1976

At the end of an assignment, when an officer is reassigned, his supervisor completes an OER for his record. Ron had asked me for information to put into my OER. Actually, he asked me to write the narrative myself. I was fine with that. I was pretty good at writing, and Ron was an unknown quantity.

The dirty little secret of Air Force OERs was that it wasn't the best officers that got promoted, it was the officers with the best-written, and endorsed, OERs. If the supervisor writing the OER was not a good word-smith, the officer being rated would be totally screwed. His career would grind to a halt through no fault of his own. So the chance to write my own OER gave me a degree of control I otherwise wouldn't have had.

And I had a lot of great things to put in my OER. I had done an excellent job managing the training of two fighter squadrons and the Suggestion Program. I had served as an IP in a mission support aircraft. I had done a great job, even though I wasn't Combat Ready, in the Koh Tang operation. I had completed all my eligible PME and my Master's Degree on my own time. And, of course, I had done a great job with Smoothflow.

Getting an endorsement from a four-star General was going to be the icing on the cake. If I could get a below-the-zone promotion to Major, my career was really on the trajectory I had envisioned when I graduated from the Academy. The assignment to Patrick was a little hiccup, but I would start working on trying to get an assignment as an Academic Instructor at the Air Force Academy as soon as I pinned on Major. As a below-the-zone Major, that shouldn't be too hard. I could follow that with another operational flying assignment, and then perhaps another staff job, this time at a major command, such as Tactical Air Command.

Yes, it looked like I had developed a good flight plan for my career.

55

March 22, 1976

Two days before my DEROS, I was in the morning staff meeting. Colonel McNeil had started a very nice, laudatory comment about my service at Kadena. Just as he was about to discuss Smoothflow, a Lieutenant Colonel rushed into the room and handed Colonel McNeil a teletype message. The Colonel stopped in mid-sentence and concentrated on the message.

"Gentlemen," he intoned, "there's been a terrible accident. General McKenzie's T-39 has crashed in Thailand." He paused and wiped his eyes, "His wife was with him on his farewell tour of Southeast Asia. There apparently was a problem stopping the aircraft on the runway, and it went off the end." He glanced down at the message again. "There is a steep drop-off at the end of the runway, and the aircraft exploded upon impact. There were no survivors."

I could immediately envision how this happened. The brakes are the weak system on the T-39. Only one pilot can apply the brakes at a time. There is a shuttle valve that allows hydraulic pressure to go to the brake system from either the pilot's brake pedals or from the copilot's, and if both pilots try to apply the brakes at the same time, the shuttle valve will be stuck in the middle, and there will be no hydraulic pressure going to the brake system. Undoubtedly, with the General in the left seat, there was an IP in the right seat, and at some point he attempted to step on the brakes at the same time as the General. And the airplane couldn't stop.

Our meeting was immediately dismissed, and a pall hung over the base the rest of the time I was at Kadena. The flags were at half-staff, and all base recreational activities were canceled.

We had been planning on leaving the base with a bang, and instead we left with a whimper.

Flying half-way around the world can be draining. Doing it with a toddler can be murder. We were traveling on a B-747 military charter flight that went from Kadena to St. Louis with a stop in Anchorage, Alaska, where we all had to deplane to go through Customs and Immigration processing. Then we waited in a large hangar while the airplane was refueled before we walked across the frozen tarmac to the boarding stairs.

Johnny was getting fidgety, and didn't want to walk. I couldn't much blame him – I felt the same way. So I ended up carrying him up the external stairs, balancing our bag of essentials on my shoulder, while Sam carried her purse and our duffel bag. By the time we got to St. Louis, we were tired, hungry, and grouchy.

And we were only half-way to our destination. We had to wait almost four hours for our flight to Orlando. When we checked in for our Trans World Airways flight, the agent told us we would not be sitting together. Clearly, that just wouldn't work.

When the cabin crew showed up at the gate, I went up to the oldest stewardess – I figured she must be the one in charge – to see if she could help us get seats together.

"Excuse me, Stewardess, can you help us?"

She looked me up and down, pausing at the ribbons on my class-A uniform.

"For starters, Captain, the word is Flight Attendant, not Stewardess. I'm Karen. What can I do for you?"

"Oops. Sorry, Karen. My wife and I are traveling with our three-year-old son, and the agent said we couldn't sit together," I said, showing her our tickets, with stick-on seat numbers attached. "Can you help us get us together?"

She turned to three young women in civvies who were wearing airline ID badges.

"Sharon, Sallie, Nancy, get over here."

They dutifully obliged.

"Show me your tickets."

They presented their tickets to Karen.

"Okay," Karen said to me, "let me see your tickets."

I handed my tickets to her, and she exchanged the seat assignment stickers from our tickers with the stickers from Sharon, Sallie and Nancy.

"They're dead-heading Flight Attendants in training," she said, "and it's no problem to re-seat them. They were going to be seated together, but I think it will be better if they get to observe from different parts of the plane. Besides," she smiled, "they're new-hires, so they won't complain."

"Thank you, Karen."

"You're welcome," she said, staring at my ribbons, "And thank you for your service."

I got a lump in my throat and started to get emotional. No one had ever said that to me. The last time I had been in the States was when I had attended Fighter Lead-In School and F-4 RTU. The war was still raging on, and anti-military sentiment had been running high. Although it had never happened to me, I had heard of returning vets being spit on. And now, I was being thanked.

I didn't know how to respond, and would have had a difficult time talking, anyway. I merely smiled and nodded, as I headed back to Sam and Johnny.

"Are you okay?" Sam asked, sensing that I was pensive.

"Yeah," I responded, blinking back tears, "I got our seats adjusted."

"So what's with the sad face?"

"The Flight Attendant just thanked me for my service."

"It's about time people thanked you," she said, as she squeezed my arm, "all of you."

56

March 23, 1976

It was dark when we arrived in Orlando, and we were dead tired.

"What do you want to do," I asked, "spend the night in a hotel and drive to Patrick tomorrow, or go there tonight?"

"Let's go there tonight and get our traveling over with," Sam answered.

"Okay."

We found the car rental concourse and walked up to the Avis counter, the only counter that didn't have a line of people waiting to be accommodated. The rental agent was a middle-age lady.

"Can I help you, sir?"

"We want to rent a car, but will need to drop it off at Satellite Beach instead of returning it here. Will that be a problem?"

"Satellite Beach…" she paused, "Are you going to Patrick Air Force Base?"

"Yes, ma'am."

She looked at the ribbons on my uniform.

"I have some of those same ribbons," she said, her bottom lip quivering, "on a plaque on my wall. The purple one and the yellow one with red stripes."

The purple ribbon was the Purple Heart Medal, and the yellow ribbon with three red stripes was the Vietnam Service Medal.

"Were you in Vietnam?" I asked.

"No, they are my son's. The ribbons are mounted on the wall … right next to my Gold Star flag." She was now fighting back tears. She took a deep breath and composed herself. "Listen, we need to reposition a sedan to Cocoa Beach, which is just up the road from Patrick."

She shuffled through a folder stuffed with rental contracts and other paperwork.

"Here," she said, as she handed me the keys and a reposition contract, "Your car is parked in the rental garage, slot H-5. Please leave it off at our Cocoa Beach office within the next week." She smiled at me as a tear trickled down her cheek, "No charge."

57

March 23, 1976

We drove right past Patrick Air Force Base without realizing it. The night was dark, and the only sign we observed directing us to Patrick Air Force Base had been about five miles earlier as we made our way south on Highway A1A from Cocoa Beach. When we saw another sign that said "You are now leaving Satellite Beach", we knew we had gone too far. We doubled back and finally found the base.

Patrick was an easy base to miss. There was no sign to direct cars to the entrance of the base. In fact, there was really no entrance to the base, no guard shack, nothing. Without a fence, the entire base was open to the public. Every road was an access point.

Since all of my operational flying had been overseas, where base security was really tight, I was mystified. I wasn't sure if this was an aberration, or if other Stateside bases were this unprotected. There were about thirty aircraft, an even mix of O-2s and OV-10s, parked on the tarmac, and I could have driven right up to them.

But, at that point, I only wanted to drive up to the

Visiting Officer Quarters and get some rest. Sam and Johnny were fast asleep in the back seat, and I couldn't wait to join them in dreamland. I found the VOQ, checked in, carried our luggage to our room, and then carried Johnny in as Sam followed me, still half asleep.

It was good to finally arrive at our destination.

58

March 25, 1976

The Base Housing Office situation was the opposite of that we experienced at Kadena. At Patrick, everyone was required to live on base, unless they received special authorization from the Squadron Commander. Some people actually wanted to live off base, so they could purchase a house and receive a housing allowance, a few hundred dollars a month. I had been living on base my entire career, and had no idea about real estate, so it was not a consideration for us. We moved into our base housing two days after we arrived.

Base housing wasn't really on base. The Capehart housing section was located five miles south of the base, in Satellite Beach. Our house was one short block from the ocean, and it was hard to tell we were in base housing, other than well-publicized requirement to keep our lawns mowed and neat.

The combined O-2 and OV-10 training squadron at Patrick Air Force Base was totally different from what I remembered from my previous O-2 training environment at Hurlburt Air Force Base. At Hurlburt, our training had been conducted at Holly Field, a small, austere subsidiary airport, and the squadron had been housed in several old quonset huts. It was intentionally sparse, to get us used to what we could expect in Vietnam.

The training squadron had moved from Hurlburt less than a year earlier, and this squadron building was a clean, modern facility. There were individual flight briefing rooms, offices, and a mass briefing room that could accommodate everyone in the squadron. When I walked into the squadron building, I felt right at home.

As soon as I reported to the Squadron Admin section, I was introduced to Major Ron Carter, the Operations Officer, and Lieutenant Colonel Stu Dillard, the Squadron Commander. They invited me into the Squadron Commander's office, and we sat on the sofa and had a nice chat. They seemed really happy to have me in the squadron.

Our mission was to train O-2 and OV-10 pilots to be Forward Air Controllers – FACs. The FAC is the eyes and ears of the fighter pilot. His job is to conduct Visual Reconnaissance of his Area of Operations and find targets. Once he finds a target, he calls the Direct Air Control Center to request fighters. When the fighters arrive, he marks the target with a willie pete rocket, and directs the fighters in their bomb deliveries.

There is a lot for a student FAC to learn. In addition to mastering the aircraft, the easy part, he must learn the capabilities of the different fighters he will employ, and the effects of the various munitions the fighters are capable of dropping.

Because I had been out of the O-2 for so long, I was going to go through the entire course, just like a brand-new student FAC. The course was easy, really easy, for me. I passed with flying colors. The O-2 IP course was more of a challenge.

Even though I had been an IP previously, in the T-39, my duties back then had been very rudimentary. Basically, all I had been required to do was babysit Generals when they wanted to fly. But now, I would be performing real instruction. Demonstration-performance instruction, and evaluating when a student would be ready to advance from one stage of training to another. And I'd be doing it all from the right seat. I found it challenging, really challenging. Finally, after going through the IP course, it was time for me to take my check ride.

59

May 4, 1976

Air Force flight check ride grading always followed a precise protocol. If a pilot met all requirements and did not require further training, he received a grade of Qualification Standard One. A Qual One didn't mean the check ride was perfect. Typically, there are numerous opportunities to make errors on a flight evaluation. As Major Runyan, my T-37 IP in Undergraduate Pilot Training, had told me, "About once a year, somewhere in the world, an Air Force pilot has a perfect check ride. Then there's the rest of us."

If a pilot met the standards but had some really glaring errors, errors that would require additional training, he received a grade of Qual Two. With a Qual Two, the pilot did not fail the check ride, and could continue operational activities, but would need some form of additional instruction to get fully up to standards. For example, perhaps he performed all the maneuvers correctly but had safe, but really lousy, landings. For corrective action, he would receive a grade of Qual Two and would be assigned additional practice performing landings. The additional practice would probably include flying with an IP and performing a specific minimum number of landings. The IP would "sign off" his additional training when his landings were satisfactory.

If the pilot had an unsatisfactory check ride, he would receive a grade of Qual Three. With a Qual Three, the pilot could not continue performing operational activities until he received additional training and re-accomplished the check ride successfully.

When I took my check ride to become an IP, I was having a bad day. A really bad day. I had been unusually tired, and had the same sort of symptoms that I'd had when I'd been diagnosed with mononucleosis back in 1973. I knew, of course, that it couldn't be mono, since I knew that people who once had mono had lifetime immunity. To be more correct, I thought I knew.

It turned out I was wrong. I once again had mono, and once again I ignored my symptoms and flew. And this time, I took a check ride. The ride was not terrible, but it sure wasn't up to my standards, especially considering the fact that I already had a lot of time flying the O-2. My range work was okay, but my landings were really lousy.

Rod, the SEFE – Stan Eval Flight Evaluator (check pilot) – assigned me a grade of Qual Two, which was totally warranted.

"You're a good IP, Ham. Your instruction on the range was excellent, and you did a great job demonstrating an ILS approach. But you really need additional practice in right seat landings. I'm giving you a grade of Qual Two, with a recommendation for Corrective Action that you perform twenty right seat landings in the next three months. As soon as you get your twenty landings, let me know, and your Corrective Action will be complete."

"In the mean time," he continued, "you can start instructing students. Just be careful, real careful, when you demo landings. You don't want to embarrass yourself."

"I think I embarrassed myself enough already," I replied, "but I agree with the grade. I've never gotten anything but a Qual One before, but I have only myself to blame."

The next day, I started working with a student who was performing some practice air strikes on the range. I wouldn't need to perform any landings, since the student would be doing the flying, and I was totally comfortable instructing in tactical operations. I was still feeling lousy, but I was in denial about having mono again. I had convinced myself that I was just worn out from the move. I decided that if I didn't feel better soon, I'd go to see the Flight Surgeon.

Two days later, Lieutenant Colonel Dillard called me into his office.

"Ham, I just received the results of your IP check

ride. Frankly, I'm really disappointed. This is a training squadron, and I can't have any IPs who have Qual Two check rides."

"Well, sir, that's the grade I received, and I think it was appropriate. My right seat landings were pretty lousy. I think getting twenty more landings will do me good."

"You'll get your twenty landings, but you'll also need to take another check ride. I'm down-grading your results to a Qual Three."

I was shocked.

"Sir, the Evaluator assigned a grade of Qual Two. That was the correct grade. The rest of the check ride went very well. I just need more work on landings."

"Perhaps you didn't understand me, Captain. I'm telling you that the only grades I will allow my IPs to receive is Qual One or Qual Three. I expect my IPs to be good enough to never require additional training."

"Colonel, you're the Squadron Commander, and you're entitled to do whatever you want. But, in my opinion, if you insist on a two-tier grading system instead of three-tier, the Evaluators will find out and will assign grades of Qual One to guys like me who could really benefit from additional training but don't deserve to fail. You're going to eventually have an accident, and it will be totally the fault of your two-tier system."

I stood up, saluted, and performed an about-face. As I got to the door of his office, I turned to face him.

"By the way, sir, you'll need to find someone to fly with Lieutenant Wayans in about an hour, since I can't fly with him if I'm unqualified."

"Well," he said, "I won't sign the downgrade until after today's mission."

"Colonel, you told me I'm unqualified. If I'm unqualified, I can't perform instructional duties."

"Besides," I said, "I'm not feeling well, and I'm on my way to the Flight Surgeon to go DNIF."

I walked out before he could respond.

60

May 15, 1976

Morale was a problem for both IPs and students. Even though Patrick was a terrific location, right on the "Space Coast" of Florida, not far from Cape Canaveral, a lot of the IPs were not thrilled with the move from Hurlburt, which was located in Fort Walton Beach. Many of them had homes they still hadn't sold, and some of them had families in Fort Walton Beach because their children were still in their schools. Fort Walton Beach was an eight-hour drive from Satellite Beach, so it was a real hardship for them.

Most of the students were really unhappy with their assignments to OV-10s or, especially, O-2s. Just like me, they wanted to get assignments to fighters. I quickly discovered that there was one common trait among all of the IPs at Patrick. They all had prior experience operating light aircraft. Many of them had worked their way through college as flight instructors. Others, such as myself, had prior experience as FACs, although all of the other guys with FAC experience had served in OV-10s. Apparently there was information in our records that indicated our prior flight time in propeller aircraft.

There was the feeling among the guys in the squadron, although no one could prove it, that the really great fighter jocks had help at their previous assignments, "sponsors", who interceded in the assignment process and kept them out of the FAC world. Those of us without sponsors felt like the dregs of the fighter world, guys who didn't warrant help from their previous Wing Commanders.

The students felt the same way, like they had been screwed getting FAC assignments. And the students were going to real operational FAC squadrons, which had the additional requirement for the FACs to work extensively with the Army. They would spend months out in the field with their assigned Army unit, living in tents and eating C-rations. Some of them would even have to become jump-qualified by attending Airborne training, Jump School, at Fort Benning, Georgia. Then, whenever their associated Army unit deployed, they would go along with them, often getting to their final location by jumping out of airplanes. All of the students felt the same: "If I wanted to play with the Army, I would have joined the Army." In the peacetime fighter pilot world, being a FAC was a shit detail.

Patrick itself was a great base. It was very compact, making it easy to walk to any office for official business. The Officers Club was outstanding. It was located right on the beach, and the dining room for their Sunday Brunch had a magnificent view. Every Sunday morning Sam, Johnny and I would have a leisurely meal as we watched the seagulls soar, glide and dive. The casual bar at the O'Club was called the Propwash. When the squadron moved down from Hurlburt, they had thrown a party there. When they entered, there were several military retirees sitting at the bar. One of the squadron guys said, "What's with all the near-deads?" and the term "near-dead" was adopted as short-hand for any of the numerous older retirees that populated the Space Coast.

When I processed in at the Patrick Consolidated Base Personnel Office, the Sergeant reviewed my records with me. This was my first opportunity to see the OER I'd received from Kadena. The narrative was glowing – naturally, since I had written it – and the endorsement was really well-written also, but was signed by the Kadena Wing Commander, a one-star General. So much for the anticipated four-star endorsement.

And so much for my plans to make Major below-the zone. When the Major Selection Board met, I was dead in the water. At nine years, I was not yet in the zone for primary promotion consideration, and with a one-button endorsement on my OER, my record didn't stand out in any way. I could see I would need to re-think my career plans.

The one really bright spot in my record, other than the combat awards, was the award I received for my service at Kadena. One day, the Squadron Admin Officer advised me that there would be an awards ceremony the next day, and I would be a recipient. When it was time for me to receive my award, I was surprised to see that I had received a Meritorious Service Medal. Normally, a MSM is only awarded to field grade officers, Major and above. In fact, it was pretty much unheard of for a Captain to receive an MSM. The MSM seemed to resurrect me in Lieutenant Colonel Dillard's eyes.

61

November 15, 1976

Maintaining morale in a peacetime FAC training squadron would be a real challenge under any circumstances. The main problem, though, was Lieutenant Colonel Dillard's lack of leadership. He was failing to exercise control over a Major who had been recently divorced, and was really into chasing women. And the real problem was that the Major's targets were some of the wives of guys in the squadron.

At squadron social functions, the Major made a habit of hitting on every female he met. Naturally, he tried to drop a hook in Sam's pond. When I heard about it, I was outraged, but Sam took it in stride.

"Honey," she said, "the guy's obviously a jerk. I can see why his wife left him. But I kind of feel sorry for him. Most important, you don't have anything to worry about."

That kind of put it in perspective for me. After hearing that, I felt a little sorry for him, but I was still pissed that Lieutenant Colonel Dillard didn't do anything about it. I was also pissed about my check ride downgrade. It was clear to me that Dillard had lost control of the squadron, and had lost the respect of the jocks

After the sleazy come-on from the Major, we decided to avoid squadron social functions, since most of them did not include children. Sam, Johnny and I were a family, and we saw no reason to break the team up just to attend an event we wouldn't enjoy.

And there were plenty of places nearby that we could enjoy. We were in Central Florida, about an hour from lots of family-oriented attractions. It took exactly 55 minutes to drive from our base house to the parking lot of the newly-opened Walt Disney World. And Disney World was a real bargain for us.

It cost exactly one dollar to enter the parking lot, and then admission to the theme park was free. Anyone who wanted to ride on an attraction had to purchase a ticket for each ride. Some rides, the tame ones, were inexpensive A-ticket rides. The more adventurous rides were the B-ticket through the most expensive, the E-ticket ride. Since Johnny was too young for most of the rides, we could have a great time at the park for very little money. Just walking around the park, and watching the Main Street parade, was enough to make a great visit.

We probably went to Walt Disney World fifty times while we were stationed at Patrick. We also visited Circus World, Sea World, Busch Gardens and Weekie

Watchie, where we could see actual mermaids perform. Okay, they were beautiful women dressed as mermaids, but it was a great show.

We settled into a lifestyle that was very comfortable. Unless we had night flying, I would leave for work at about 0700 and get home at 1700. During the summer, when the days were long, we would walk to the beach after I returned from flying. And every day Sam and I took turns watching Johnny while we ran along the beach in turn. Altogether, it was an idyllic time.

Professionally, I was enjoying my work. I had become a SEFE, and enjoyed administering check rides. I liked see a guy who was putting on his best performance. And I really enjoyed seeing the looks on my students' faces when we went to the tactical range. Until that point in their training, they were just pissed off about their assignments. But once they controlled actual fighters in simulated combat, they would return with shit-eating grins.

The fighters we worked with were active-duty and Air National Guard fighter units who would come to Patrick TDY for a week at a time to get experience working with FACs on Avon Park Range. It was a win-win; the fighters got to work with a real FAC, and our students got to work with real fighters. Every now and then I'd run into a fighter jock I knew when he would cycle through Patrick.

Toward the end of the year, Sam and I decided that Johnny should have a brother or sister.

62

May 8, 1977

My mother and my dad's war buddy Phil had driven down from Pensacola a few days earlier to visit us and help out while Sam was in the hospital. Sam was approaching nine months into her pregnancy, and had experienced several episodes of false alarms. After hearing about the problems during the previous pregnancy, our doctor wanted to keep her under continuous observation until her delivery.

Johnny's feet hardly touched the ground the whole time Mom and Phil were visiting – they were constantly picking him up, pinching his cheeks, playing with him. He wasn't used to the constant attention from anyone other than Sam and me, and was really enjoying it.

My mother was making breakfast when I walked into the kitchen.

"Happy Mother's Day," I said, as I gave her a big hug and kissed her on the cheek.

"Thank you. This is my best Mother's Day ever, getting to spend time with my grandson."

"I'm going to head out to the hospital to give Sam

her Mother's Day present," I said, as I showed Mom the box of Whitman's Sampler candy I'd gotten at the BX.

"I think she'll love it, and..." She was interrupted by the ringing of the telephone.

I ran over and picked it up on the first ring.

"This is Doctor Weatherby," the voice on the other end said, "It's time."

"I'll be there in ten minutes."

"Don't worry," Mom said, "we'll watch Johnny. Get going!"

I got into my car, turned on the emergency flashers, and sped up South Patrick Drive to the Base Hospital. I arrived just as they were wheeling Sam into the Delivery Room. I quickly scrubbed and donned a gown.

Sam looked really relieved to see me. Her contractions were coming closer together, and I was able to offer more help this time than previously. She was in labor for a little under three hours and produced another son for me. I was starting to feel like an old hand when I cut the cord this time, but I still cried, a lot, as I held my newborn son. I carried him over to Sam.

She held out her arms.

"Let me hold Tommy."

"So his name is Thomas?"

"Yes. Thomas Jefferson Hancock. You know how Thomas Jefferson relates to John Adams, right?"

"Sure," I replied, "I've been studying my American History. They were both signers of the Declaration of Independence, and both early presidents."

"That's the grade school answer. Give me the college level answer."

"Not sure."

"Thomas Jefferson died on the same day as his former arch enemy, John Adams."

"The Fourth of July?"

"Yes. Fifty years to the day after signing the Declaration of Independence. They had buried the hatchet before they died."

"That's really amazing. So," I looked at her, "what name were you going to use if we'd had a daughter?"

"You'll see when we have our daughter."

I gave Sam and our newest family member a gentle hug.

"Happy Mother's Day, Darling."

63

October 10, 1977

The one thing I hadn't anticipated about being an RTU IP was the repetition, the monotony. Unlike all of my previous flying, where every mission was different, most of the missions I flew at Patrick were pretty much the same. They were either local Qualification sorties, Navigation sorties, or range rides. The Qual sorties consisted of instrument approaches and landing practice. The Nav sorties provided the students with training reading and flying with reference to 1-to-50 charts. On a 1-to-50 chart, one inch on the map represents fifty thousand inches on the ground. It was a perfect chart for navigating as a FAC.

Range rides consisted of either firing willie pete rockets at the target on the scorable range, or conducting simulated air strikes against targets on the tactical range, simulating combat. So there was a bit of variety, but after taking 30 or 40 students through various stages of training, it started to get old, really old. We always took off and landed at the same airport.

Almost always. On one mission to the tactical range, we were in the middle of a simulated air strike when I saw a sudden drop in the indication on the rear engine Fuel Flow gauge. The Fuel Flow gauge was actually a fuel pressure indicator, and a sudden drop would indicate a broken fuel line, which could cause a fire.

The Emergency Procedure for a sudden fuel flow drop was to instantly shut down the engine and feather the propeller.

"I have the airplane," I said, as I went through the required actions. The rear engine on the O-2 is the critical engine. In fact, the Service Ceiling when operating on only the front engine is 4000 feet below the Service Ceiling when operating on only the rear engine. And, on this particular hot Florida day, the front-engine-only Service Ceiling was only 100 feet MSL, and the terrain in the vicinity of the Avon Park range was about 100 feet MSL, with trees extending another 80 feet.

We were at about 1000 feet when we shut down the engine, and the aircraft could not maintain altitude. At that altitude we were too low, too close to the trees, to see the emergency airfield located at the town of Avon Park, but I knew the direction for an emergency diversion from the range. I took up a heading of 280, looked below the aircraft to ensure the area was uninhabited, and jettisoned the rocket pods.

We were drifting down at about 100 feet per minute, and there was a real question about whether we would make the airfield before we ran out of altitude. I could see a treeless area up ahead where the airport was located, but still couldn't see the runway due to the trees. Finally, runway 28 came into view, directly in front of us. I waited until I was sure I would make it, then I lowered the gear and landed on "brick one". After I landed, I taxied to the ramp and shut down. It reminded me a lot of my emergency landing at Saravane, in Laos, in 1969. It was nice to be back on the ground, and it was also cool to land somewhere other than Patrick Air Force Base.

I had another very memorable mission. I was taking a student out on a Navigation mission, and the lesson plan called for practice using binoculars to locate targets on the ground. It was a hot day, there were a lot of thermals making the airplane very unstable, and it was extremely difficult to keep the target in the binocular field of view.

To make matters worse, my student had been up all night, driving back from a bar he had been at in Jacksonville, celebrating after watching a football game the previous day, a Sunday. He was hung over, and, in retrospect, someone should have prevented him from flying. That someone should have been me. But I didn't realize he was in such bad shape until we were already airborne.

I showed him how to use binoculars, how to keep track of a target on the ground while still flying the airplane, and how to locate the target on the map. I thought he could handle it. I thought wrong. He lowered the binoculars from his eyes, turned to me, and said, "I think I'm going to...".

And then he threw up, all over himself. But at least it didn't get on me. It didn't get on me until he opened his fresh air vent, which allowed outside air to enter the cockpit. He opened his vent, fresh air entered at 120 knots, and his vomit sprayed all over the cockpit. And all over me. We terminated our mission, of course, returned to Patrick, and got clean by getting hosed down by the Fire Department.

64

March 12, 1978

Because of my previous experience in the O-2, I was pretty much considered the squadron expert in all things relating to the airplane. A few of the other IPs in the squadron had flown in Vietnam, but their experience had been in other airplanes. Some were fighter jocks, some had flown as FACs in OV-10s, but nobody else had flown the O-2 in combat. So it was pretty natural for me to be assigned an additional duty as Flight Manual Review Officer.

The O-2A Dash One was officially called Technical Order 1-O2A-1. The Dash One was the final word on anything relating to the systems or operation of the airplane. Whenever a system was changed, or a procedure was amended, the Dash One was revised. Even with the airplane already a mature airframe, having been in Air Force service for over ten years, there were still changes that required issuing a revised Dash One. Sometimes the changes were small, basically word-smithing issues. Some other changes were more significant.

Whenever the Dash One needed an immediate change, a notice would go out to all the pilots to make a pen-and-ink change to the copy that each pilot owned. After a while, it seemed like almost every page had some annotations, and when it got bad enough, a new Dash One would be produced, incorporating all the previous pen-and-ink changes.

As a final quality control filter, all the major stakeholders would send attendees to a Dash One Review Conference to go over all the proposed changes. One representative from each operational squadron, plus a conference leader from Tactical Air Command Headquarters, would go over every page of the Dash One in detail. Even though the Dash One was only a few hundred pages, the process usually took an entire week.

This year, the Dash One Conference was being held in Denver, and I was the representative from our squadron. I was looking forward to getting back to Colorado, since I hadn't been there since my graduation from the Academy. I had a rental car reserved, and planned to drive down to Colorado Springs during my free time, if there was any. This was going to be a nice trip down memory lane.

Patrick Air Force Base was an easy one-hour drive to the Orlando airport, and Sam drove me, with Johnny and Tommy safely in car seats in the back. This was going to be the first time I'd be spending any time away from home since arriving at Patrick. It was a strange feeling.

"Are you sure you're going to be okay while I'm away?" I asked, even though I already knew the answer.

"I think we'll manage," Sam smiled, "and I think you need to go back and visit your roots."

"Okay. You have the hotel's number if you need to get in touch with me, and I'll call every night."

It occurred to me that this was the first time in Tommy's entire life that I wouldn't be there to tuck him into his crib. I leaned into the back seat and kissed Johnny on his cheek, and then kissed Tommy on his forehead. Tommy looked at me and, probably sensing my tension, started to cry.

"He'll be okay," Sam said, "I'll have him giggling in a few minutes."

Then she held me tightly and gave me a warm kiss.

"This, plus last night, will have to hold you over until you get back."

It had been a challenge finding time for any intimate moments ever since the kids were born. But the previous night we had found the time, recreating the tradition we'd established ever since we were based together, at Yokota. Whenever I would leave for a TDY assignment, we'd made a point of having one last lovemaking session the night before my departure. It was nice to keep up the tradition.

As I walked into the terminal, I gave one last look back and saw Sam already driving away. Yeah, they'd be okay while I was away.

I was a bit early for flight check-in, so I went into one of the restaurants in the terminal. Sam had cooked me a great breakfast before we left home, so I bypassed the breakfast buffet and sat at the counter. I ordered a cup of coffee and looked around. Off in the corner, I saw a pilot and copilot helping themselves to seconds, or perhaps thirds, from the buffet. The Captain, the pilot with four stripes on his sleeve, looked to be about five years older than I was, while the copilot, with three stripes, looked about my age. I wondered if they were going to be operating my flight.

It didn't take long for me to find out. After I finished my coffee I went to the gate to wait for my flight, and saw the same pilots at the podium talking to the agent. Then they went through the access door on the loading bridge. I suspected they might have been former military pilots, since they looked in my direction several times, and it appeared to me that the Captain gave me a slight nod.

I would have preferred to have traveled in civvies, but the rules were that we needed to be in our Class-A uniforms whenever we traveled on an airline flight. Personally, if I had to travel in uniform I would have preferred a flight suit, but rules are rules. Judging by the appearance of the other passengers, I would be the only active-duty military passenger on the flight.

Finally it was nearing time to board. I heard my name being announced by the agent, and as I approached her at the podium, she said there would be a seat change for me, holding out her hand for me to surrender my boarding pass. A seat change was fine with me, since I had been assigned seat 15B, a middle seat. When I received my new boarding pass, I saw I was assigned seat 2B.

"Is this another middle seat?" I asked.

"No," the agent smiled, "it's an aisle seat in First Class. The Captain said we needed to move you forward for weight-and-balance purposes."

I was speechless. I had never been in First Class before, and this was going to be a real treat. I made a mental note to personally thank the Captain after the flight. When it was time to board, the agent enplaned those of us in First Class ahead of the other passengers. There were only three rows of First Class seats, and I couldn't believe how luxurious the seats were. They were large, leather seats, and I estimated they had twice the legroom of the normal Economy seats. Now *this* was the manner to which I would like to become accustomed!

As soon as I was settled into my seat, a Flight Attendant approached me.

"Good morning, Mr. Hancock. I'm Nancy Walters, the Purser. Would you care for a beverage before departure?"

Apparently she had gotten my name from the passenger manifest, which had obviously been updated when my seat was reassigned. I glanced around and saw that another passenger in First Class was having a cocktail. Free drinks, I didn't need to drive, I wouldn't overdo it, and Sam would never have to know.

But a deal is a deal. I remember Dad telling me that integrity is doing the right thing when no one is watching.

"Thank you. I'd just like an orange juice, please," I replied.

After a short wait the Flight Attendant brought my OJ, and handed me a menu.

"What is your preference for the in-flight meal, Mr. Hancock?"

I looked at the menu. There was a choice of an omelet, a fruit plate, a cheese plate, and yogurt.

"I think I'll have the omelet, please."

"Yes, sir. We'll be serving as soon as we reach cruising altitude."

"Thank you."

As the Economy section passengers boarded, I couldn't help noticing their envious glances as they passed through the First Class section. I wondered if that was the way I behaved when I boarded commercial flights. I tried to look nonchalant, as though I was totally experienced with traveling in First Class. I think the shit-eating-grin on my face gave me away.

Shortly after takeoff, the Flight Attendant started the breakfast service. She lowered my tray table and covered it with a small white linen tablecloth. Then she brought my meal, and poured me a cup of coffee. The entire meal was served on real china, including the coffee cup. Now *this* was the way to travel. No Styrofoam cups and plastic serving trays on this flight.

After breakfast, I leaned back my seat, closed my eyes, and was gently rocked to sleep by the rhythmic undulations of the flight. At some point, Nancy covered me with a warm blanket.

Yes, this was the way to fly.

65

March 12, 1978

Nancy was shaking me. I smiled and opened my eyes, expecting to see the pleasant Flight Attendant offering me another round of food, or perhaps a refill on my coffee. She looked scared.

"Are you a pilot, Mr. Hancock?"

"Yes," I responded, unconsciously touching the wings on the left chest of my Class-A uniform. I was fully awake now, and could see the terror in her eyes.

"You're needed at the flight deck, *now*!"

I unbuckled my seat belt and followed her to the cramped cockpit. As soon as she opened the door, I was overcome by the sickening smell of vomit. The Captain and First Officer were in their seats, slumped forward, held in their positions by their seat belts and shoulder harnesses. They appeared to be totally unconscious. They each were covered with vomit, as was the center instrument pedestal.

"The Captain called me a few minutes ago and said they were both feeling ill," the Nancy said. "When I came back up with some club soda, I found them like this. Can you fly this airplane?"

"I guess I can," I replied, "what kind of airplane is this, and where are we?"

"It's a 737-200," she had a stern look, "I announced that during the safety briefing. We're somewhere over western Kansas. About fifteen minutes ago the Captain told me we would be starting our descent soon. Then this."

"Okay. Help me get these guys out of their seats, and then stay up here with me."

Since the airplane was still flying along smoothly, it was clear we were on autopilot. I'd never used an autopilot before, and I had no idea how to operate it or disconnect it to hand-fly.

First things first. We needed to get these guys out of their seats. I started with the First Officer, since he looked to be the lightest. I reached around and tried to unlock his shoulder harness and seat belt, which were fastened together in a large round buckle at his waist. I couldn't find any kind of release lever or button.

"Twist the center to release it," Nancy suggested.

I grabbed the hub of the buckle and turned it, first to the right. It didn't move. Then I turned it to the left and the harness and seat belt released. I needed to lift him out of the seat, but I couldn't stand up straight, and it was very awkward trying to lift from this angle. I tensed my core muscles and reached under his arms. As I lifted, to try to move him out of the seat, the left arm rest was blocking my way.

Nancy reached around me and raised the arm rest out of the way.

"Thanks."

I dragged the First Officer out of his seat, pulling rather than lifting, and moved him to the galley area outside the cockpit. As I went back to get the Captain, I glanced back and saw the terrified looks of the First Class passengers. No time for explanations, I headed back up to the cockpit to get the Captain.

Nancy helped me with the Captain, and then brought up some towels to try to wipe the mess off the controls.

I sat down in the Captain's seat and looked around. This shouldn't be so difficult. An airplane is an airplane is an airplane. The instruments all were familiar, the same cluster we had in the T-39. The throttles were in the same place as in the T-39. Okay, there was the gear handle, right where it should be. I looked outside, and was relieved to see it was a clear day. Things were looking up. But I had to find out where we were, and figure out how to disconnect the autopilot.

The speaker in the overhead panel crackled,

"WorldJet Airways 338, Denver, descend at pilot discretion to one-five thousand feet. Altimeter two niner niner four."

I looked at the Flight Attendant. "Is that us?"

"Yes, we're WorldJet Flight 338."

I looked around to find a headset or microphone. The headset was hanging on a hook just above the left side window. That explained why the cockpit speaker was turned on. Apparently, the crew was using a hand microphone and cockpit speaker while at cruising altitude.

"WorldJet Airways 338, acknowledge."

I put on the headset and felt around the horns of the control yoke to find the Transmit switch. There it was, on the front of the left horn of the yoke.

"Mayday, mayday, mayday," I transmitted, "This is WorldJet 338 declaring an emergency. Both pilots are totally incapacitated, and I'm one of the passengers at the controls."

The controller came back immediately, sounding totally professional, as though he'd handled this a thousand times.

"Roger WorldJet 338. Have you ever flown an aircraft before?"

"That's affirmative," I replied, "I'm an Air Force pilot."

"Well I guess this is our lucky day," he commented. He sounded really relieved. "Do you have any experience in large aircraft?"

"I've flown the T-29, and the F-4. Both have a gross weight of approximately 50,000 pounds."

"Okay, we're working on getting a 737 Instructor Pilot on frequency to talk you through what you need to do. It will be a few minutes before he's up on frequency. You're well within our service volume area, so we'll be giving you a single frequency approach and staying with you all the way."

"Thank you." I was starting to relax a little now. I had gotten used to the smell of vomit, I was at the controls of an airplane that was starting to feel a little more comfortable, and I had no trouble interpreting the airplane instruments.

Now all I had to do was figure out how to disconnect the damn autopilot.

66

March 12, 1978

We were cruising at 33,000, Flight Level 330. Clearly, we needed to descend, and soon.

As I surveyed the cockpit, I noticed a panel above the center instrument cluster that was totally unfamiliar to me. There were two flat paddle-like switches, and a small window that currently read "33000". Obviously, this was an altitude reminder, possibly an altitude reporter.

To the left of the throttles there was a large lever, labeled "Speed Brake". Okay, I knew what a speed brake was. We used to stuff chaff in the speed brakes of the F-4, and I'd used them when I had tons of overtake during rejoins in the F-4. Nothing new there.

"Denver," I transmitted, "any luck getting an IP on freq? I'm trying to figure out how to get the autopilot to let go, so I can start a descent."

"Roger, WorldJet 338. We expect him to be up on frequency any minute. I want you to remain on this frequency, and we're going to clear everyone else off."

"Roger."

"Attention all aircraft," Denver Center transmitted, "all aircraft except WorldJet 338 contact Denver Center on frequency 124.7. Do not acknowledge." There was a short pause. "Okay, WorldJet, you have my undivided attention, and we will dispense with the call signs."

"Roger."

A different voice came up on the radio.

"WorldJet 338, this is Captain Fisher. I'm an IP with WorldJet Airways, and I'm going to give you your first lesson in flying the Guppy."

"The what?" I asked.

"Sorry. We call the 737 the Guppy. Airline humor. Anyway, they tell me you have some experience as a pilot, is that right?"

"Yes, I'm in the Air Force and have 3300 hours. Tactical aircraft, plus T-29s and T-39s."

"Okay, this should be a piece of cake for you. Consider this a big T-29. But be careful with power management. The engines are under-slung, so the nose will pitch up when you add power, and it will drop when you pull off power."

"Got it."

"What's your name, WorldJet?"

"Hamilton."

"Okay, Hamilton, you can call me Tom. I'm former Air Force also, and I can tell we're going to get along just fine. First order of business is disconnecting the autopilot and starting you on your descent. Above the center instrument panel is a horizontal panel we call the Mode Control Panel. Do you see it?"

"The one with the paddles and the altitude reminder?"

"That's the one. First, I want you to dial in fifteen thousand in the Altitude Alerter. Then I'm going to have you disconnect the autopilot and start a hand-flown descent."

As he was speaking, I dialed in 15000 into the small window.

"The Autopilot Disconnect Switch is a small button on the left horn of your yoke. Do you see it?"

"Yes, Tom, I see it," I said, as I pressed the button.

"Don't press it yet, until I warn you..."

Too late! The two paddle switches on the Mode Control Panel snapped down, a loud intermittent siren was repeatedly sounding in the cockpit, and a red light was flashing on the forward instrument panel. I was startled, and Nancy, who had by now taken a position in the First Officer seat, looked terrified.

"I already pressed it!"

"Okay," he said, "I can hear the horn in the back ground. Press the button again."

I pressed the button again, and the siren stopped blaring and the light stopped flashing. Now I was flying an airplane. Like Tom said, a big T-29.

"I'm departing Flight Level 330 for one-five thousand," I transmitted.

Another voice came on the radio, "Descend now to one-one thousand."

"Roger." I dialed 11000 into the Altitude Alerter.

"Now Hamilton," Tom said, I want you to descend at point seven-seven Mach until you reach 270 knots, then continue to descend at 270."

"Roger, I can do that." The instruments looked totally familiar to me from my days flying the T-39. Quite different from the instrument cluster on the O-2, but my instrument scan came back quickly. Like riding a bike. I pulled the throttles to Idle and gently extended the Speed Brake. I wanted to get the feel for the airplane as quickly as I could, and I could best do that in the thicker air at lower altitude.

"Hamilton, what aircraft are you flying in the Air Force right now?"

"The O-2A. It's a small aircraft, actually it's a Cessna 337."

"I have time in O-2s also," Tom responded, "I flew them when we first got them in the inventory. I was based at DaNang."

"Small world. I was at DaNang also, in 1969. What did you say your name was?"

"Tom Fisher… wait a minute! Hamilton, Hamilton … Hamfist! Is that you? This is Fish, your old roomie!"

I had thought the voice sounded familiar. This was Fish Fisher, my room-mate from DaNang!

By this time, the Nancy was sitting with her mouth agape, an incredulous look on her face. I couldn't help myself, I had to say the inside joke Fish and I had used ever since he came back from Australia on R&R.

"Fish," I transmitted, "was I brought here to die?"

"No, mite," he replied, "you was brought here yesti'die."

By this time, Nancy was absolutely dumbfounded. I was laughing hysterically, and was totally relaxed.

"What the fuck is the matter with the two of you?" she demanded, incredulously.

"Inside joke," I said. Then it occurred to me that

there were probably twenty other people still on frequency, and they probably thought the two of us were absolutely crazy.

As if on cue, Fish and I became totally serious, as he talked me through how to maneuver the 737. He had me perform a constant-rate descent using the Instantaneous Vertical Speed Indicator, some turns to headings, and some airspeed variations, managing the effects of power on pitch . Other than the IVSI being much more sensitive and responsive than the Vertical Speed Indicator on the Air Force airplanes I'd flown, it was pretty much a piece of cake.

The proof, of course, would be in the landing.

67

March 12, 1978

I had been getting vectors from Denver Center, and they handed me off to Denver Approach Control, all on the same frequency. Fish had been giving me flying lessons along the way. At one point, I discovered my feet couldn't reach the rudder pedals.

"There's a crank below the instrument panel, right between your legs," Fish said. "Do you see it?"

I found the crank and turned it, first clockwise, which didn't help, then counter-clockwise. The rudder pedals moved back to meet me, and my seat was finally adjusted to where it needed to be.

We were now at 8000 feet, 210 knots, heading toward Stapleton Airport.

"Denver Airport at your 12 o'clock seven miles," Approach Control announced, "Runway 35 Right is the longest, at 12,000 feet. Wind calm. Tower advises you are cleared to land."

"Airport in sight," I responded. Approach Control had vectored me onto a long straight-in final approach.

"Okay, Hamfist," Fish said, "now comes the fun part. I want you to set both fuel flows to 3000."

I adjusted the throttles until the Fuel Flow Indicators read 3000 pounds per hour.

"Now," he continued, "I want to let you know, the Guppy has JT-8-D engines. They don't have the instantaneous response you're used to. You really need to stay on top of airspeed control. The quicker you make a response, the smaller it can be."

"Roger."

"I want you to select Flaps One. First, press the Horn Silence button at the back of the throttle quadrant."

I found the Horn Silence button and pressed it. "Nancy," I said, gesturing toward the Flap Lever, "give me Flaps One."

"It won't move," she said, as she wiggled the handle.

I tried to move it, and it appeared stuck.

"The flap handle won't move," I transmitted.

"You have to lift it. Try lifting it, then move it into the Flaps One detent."

Nancy pulled up on the handle, and then moved it

to the Flaps One detent. The aircraft pitched over slightly, and I gave a few clicks of nose-up trim. Fish had earlier alerted me to the surprising noise of the large trim wheel that loudly rotated with every click of the trim button.

"Okay," Fish transmitted, "the airspeed should stabilize around 190."

We were at 193 knots.

"Roger that," I replied.

"Now," Fish said, "go to Flaps Five."

Nancy selected Flaps Five.

"Do you see the VASI?" Fish asked.

The Visual Approach Slope Indicator is a set of lights alongside the runway that indicate the airplane'?s position on a visual glide path.

"Affirmative. Right now it's red over pink".

"Okay, go gear down and Flaps Fifteen now. When you get red over white, go to Flaps Thirty and lower your nose three degrees. Use a base fuel flow of 3000, make small throttle movements, and stay in trim."

"Roger."

"Gear down," I said to Nancy, "and Flaps Fifteen." Nancy dutifully put the gear handle to the Down position and lowered the flaps another notch. I kept trimming to hold the airplane in level flight.

Finally, the VASI showed red over white, the "on glide slope" indication.

"Flaps Thirty." I lowered the nose three degrees and trimmed.

"You want to maintain 130 knots," fish said, "but a few knots plus or minus is okay. It's more important for you to stay on the glide path. Your ground speed will be about 140, so I want you to descend at half your ground speed times ten. Shoot for 700 feet per minute down."

"Okay."

"Now," Fish continued, "do you see the Radio Altimeter? It's next to the Altimeter."

I hadn't noticed it until now, probably because it only indicated radio altitudes of less than 1000 feet, and the needle was not yet in view.

"Yes."

"Okay, Hamfist, I'm going to talk you through a mechanical way to land the Guppy. When the Radio Altimeter reads 30 feet, I want you to gently flare the airplane, looking at the far end of the runway."

"All right, but I may have some trouble looking outside and also looking at the Radio Altimeter."

"You said you had the Flight Attendant in the cockpit, is that right?"

"Affirm."

"Have her call the 30 feet for you."

I glanced over at Nancy, and pointed at the Radio Altimeter.

"Do you think you can handle that, Nancy? Just call out the altitudes as we get close to the ground."

"I think I can do it," she replied.

"Okay," I transmitted, "we have a handle on it."

"Last thing," Fish said. "After you land, just stop straight ahead on the runway. Raise the Reverser Levers after you land, and use your wheel brakes. Don't try to taxi clear. You don't have complete steering authority with the rudder pedals. We use the tiller to steer, and it's really sensitive. So just stop wherever you can, and we'll have stairs ready to meet the airplane. The parking brake is set with the small lever just to the left of the throttle quadrant. To set the parking brake, just step on the brakes and raise that lever."

"Got it."

We were now on final approach. I gave a last glance inside the airplane and checked my airspeed. It was steady at 130 knots.

We passed over the approach lights, and I was precisely on the VASI. Out of the corner of my eye, I saw the Radio Altimeter pass through 100 feet.

"Talk to me, Nancy."

"Eighty," she replied, "seventy, sixty, fifty, forty, thirty..."

I gently flared the aircraft, looking at the far end of the runway, as I pulled the throttles to Idle. The wheels gave a short chirp as the airplane landed. A cheer erupted from the back of the airplane as I brought it to a stop.

"Great job, Hamfist!" Fish yelled, "Now pull the Fuel Control Levers, below the throttles, to Cut-Off. I'll meet you planeside."

I positioned the Fuel Control Levers to Cut-Off, and heard the engines winding down. Then all of the instruments died and the aircraft suddenly became strangely quiet, the only sound the whirring of the gyros as they spun down.

We were safe on the runway, and I could see emergency response vehicles approaching us. Nancy was crying now, and unstrapped from the First Officer seat and hugged me tightly.

"Thank you, thank you, thank you!"

"You're welcome, Nancy. I couldn't have done it

without your help."

She blinked back tears, straightened her uniform and turned toward the cockpit door. She appeared a little embarrassed.

"I need to go disarm the slide at Door One Left."

Mobile stairs had been positioned at the front entry door, and medics rushed aboard as soon as the door was opened. They immediately inserted IV drips into the Captain and First Officer, stabilized their condition, and removed them to the waiting ambulance.

Nancy had made a PA announcement asking the passengers to remain seated until the medics deplaned, and everyone complied. After the medics left, Nancy instructed the passengers to gather their personal belongings, and to exit the airplane through the same door where they had entered. Buses were waiting to transport them to the terminal. At the same time, mechanics were hooking a tow vehicle to the airplane nose wheel.

As the passengers deplaned, almost all of them looked up into the cockpit and thanked me. It was a really satisfying feeling. If I hadn't been on board, I don't know what would have happened.

I had an instantaneous flash back to high school Latin class. We had been translating some really difficult passages, and I still remembered the quote from the Roman philosopher Seneca. *Fortuna est momentum quo occasionem convenit talentum*: "Luck is what happens when preparation meets opportunity".

Today I'd had my share of luck.

68

March 12, 1978

I waited for all the passengers to leave, and then I went back to seat 2B, retrieved my carry-on bag, and descended the portable stairs. There was a throng of reporters all trying to get my attention, and I felt very uncomfortable being in the spotlight. A reporter from a news team shoved a microphone in front of me.

"What's it feel like, being the hero that saved the plane?"

I paused for a moment to collect my thoughts.

"I'm not a hero. I'm just a pilot, doing what I was trained to do. But I've served with a lot of heroes. Fifty-eight thousand of them."

As I was trying to think of something else to say, I saw Fish drive up in a van with the WorldJet Airways logo on the side. He was out of the vehicle as soon as the parking brake was set, and ran up to me and gave me a bear hug that knocked the wind out of me.

"Great job, Hamfist! You are one hell of a pilot!"

"I think it was because you are one hell of an

instructor." I replied. "Once again you save the bacon."

Fish had pulled my ass out of the fire more than once when we were at DaNang. The first time, he covered for me when I was making a drunken fool of myself. More important, he flew res-cap – rescue cover – for me when I was shot down in Laos.

"So how did you get to be such a big shot in your airline?"

"Climb in," he said, heading toward the van, "and I'll tell you all about it. And can you *please* take off that uniform blouse? You smell like a barf bag."

"I know. Reminds me of our drinking days at DaNang."

I removed my Class-A uniform jacket, folded it, inside out, and put it in the back seat.

"How about you stay at my house? I want you to meet my wife, anyway."

"Thanks, but I don't know, Fish. I'm here for a Dash One conference that's being held at my hotel. I think I should stay there. But we could do dinner together."

"Okay, I'll call Rachel and tell her to get ready. Where are you staying?"

"The Stapleton Doubletree."

"All right. Let's get you checked in, then we'll go out to lunch. You can do that, can't you?"

"Absolutely. I don't need to meet up with the attendees until tomorrow morning."

Fish parked the airline van in front of airline headquarters, at the rear entrance of the terminal, and we transferred to his Toyota. He drove me to the Doubletree, which was only a block from the airport, and I quickly checked in and changed into civvies. I removed the ribbons and insignia from my uniform, put it into the plastic laundry bag I found in the closet, and left the bag outside my room door. Then I called the front desk to tell them I had a rush dry cleaning job for pickup.

"Okay, Fish, I'm all yours."

"Let's go," Fish answered, as we walked across the parking lot to his car, "What kind of food are you in the mood for?"

"I haven't had sushi in over two years." I remembered hearing that a lot of Japanese had been relocated to internment camps in Colorado during the war, and there was a Little Tokyo section in Denver.

"I know just the place. So you like sushi... Did you ever hook up with that Japanese girl?"

"You have a good memory," I said, as I took my

family photos out of my wallet, "Actually, she's Eurasian."

Fish stopped walking and stared at the pictures.

"Wow! I *wish* she was my Asian! You really lucked out."

"I know. I sure got the best part of the bargain, that's for sure. That's Samantha, and our boys, Johnny and Tommy. We got married a year after I left DaNang."

We made small talk as we drove the short distance to downtown Denver.

"What I really like about Stapleton is how close it is to downtown," Fish commented, as he parked in a vacant spot on Champa Street, "And what I like about Denver is how compact the city is. You can walk just about anywhere. This is probably the best pilot base in the entire system."

We walked a short distance.

"How's this?" he asked, as we stopped in front of a small sign that read "Sakura Sushi".

"Looks perfect."

We entered a small restaurant and waited for the hostess to seat us.

"*Futari, onegai-shimasu,*" I said, in my best

Japanese. I wasn't sure who I was trying to impress more, Fish or the hostess.

"*Hai, dozo,*" she responded, leading us to a table in the corner.

We glanced over the menu, and I picked out what I wanted.

"So," Fish said, "fill me in on the past nine years."

"Well, after DaNang, I went to Yokota to fly T-39s."

"So you didn't get the B-52 deal like the rest of us."

"No, I lucked out. I married Sam while I was at Yokota. I ended up going TDY to Vietnam a lot, then volunteered for a second tour."

"Wow. You really are a lifer, aren't you. What did you fly your second tour?"

"F-4s. I got to Ubon just in time for Linebacker, and DEROSed just as the POWs were coming home. Perfect timing."

"I'll say."

"Then I went to Kadena in F-4s."

I wanted to tell him about my aerial victories, but I thought better of it. I didn't want to sound like I was bragging.

"I flew F-4s for a little while, then they put me in Wing Ops and Training, and I ended up flying T-29s for a short time, then T-39s again. Actually, I was dual qualified, so I flew the F-4 also."

"Wow. Very cool."

"After that, they sent me to Patrick to be an O-2 IP. How about you? As I recall, you went to Buffs."

The "as I recall" part was a polite bit of an understatement. The last month he was at DaNang, all Fish could talk about was how badly he'd been screwed over by MPC with his B-52 assignment.

"Let me tell you, Hamfist," Fish grinned, "that B-52 assignment was the best thing that ever happened to me."

"You're shitting me, right?"

"No, it was my entrance into flying heavy metal. If I hadn't gotten that Buff assignment, I wouldn't be where I am today. I learned how to operate in a crew environment, I learned a lot more about jet engines than we learned in pilot training, and I learned about Boeing systems and procedures. Most important, I met my wife while I was at Castle Air Force Base, going through training."

"I had a DOS (Date of Separation)," he continued, "and WorldJet was just starting to hire when I got out of the Air Force. I went to the interview and dazzled them with my knowledge of how the big Boeings operate, and I was in the first new-hire class."

"Very cool," I responded.

"Here's the best part. With the big hiring and expansion, I made Captain in less than six years. Some of the guys I few with when I was first hired took fifteen years or more to upgrade. Like they say, timing is everything."

"How did you get to be an IP?"

"Well, in the airline, seniority is everything. Totally different from the Air Force, where guys upgrade based on ability. The one place where they hire based on performance rather than seniority is in the Training Department. I had been doing a pretty good job on the line, and my Chief Pilot invited me to apply for a position as an IP."

"Impressive."

"I don't know. More luck than anything. So, I interviewed with the Training Department and some personnel types, went through additional training, and became a 737 IP. I work in the Training Center seventeen days a month, and fly three days. Every third month I fly the line the whole month just like a normal pilot." Fish paused for effect. "During a typical line month I have eighteen days off."

He was grinning like a Cheshire cat.

I was incredulous. "Eighteen days a month of work, or eighteen days a month off?"

"Eighteen days *off*. That's what the line guys get. And if the bullshit level at the Training Center ever gets too deep, I can go back to line flying whenever I want."

The waitress had brought our order and placed it on the table between us.

"So," Fish said, "what's the deal here? Do we eat with our fingers, chopsticks, what?"

"We use chopsticks, called *hashi*. Here, I'll show you."

Fish and I spent about an hour at the restaurant, with me showing him how to use *hashi*, and him telling me about airline life. It was really great to be back with Fish again, and to see the good old Fish, the happy, vibrant guy he had been when I'd first met him at DaNang. I could see that airline life agreed with him. It sounded like a great lifestyle.

After lunch, Fish took me to the car rental desk at Stapleton, and we made arrangements to have dinner at his house in Castle Rock at five o'clock.

69

March 12, 1978

When I was a cadet at the Air Force Academy, Castle Rock had been just a wide spot in the road. Actually, it was just off the road, on the east side of I-25. As seniors, when we were allowed to have cars, we knew we were getting close to the North Gate of the Academy when we passed the Castle Rock exit on our way back from Denver. The giant prominence that gave the town its name was easy to spot from miles away. The fastest I ever made it from Castle Rock to the North Gate was seventeen minutes. One guy, who had a Corvette, claimed he had done it in eleven.

Castle Rock was different now. Larger. Much larger. There were lots of winding roads that hadn't existed when I was a cadet. The hills on the east side of the highway were dotted with gorgeous homes overlooking the town. I followed the directions Fish had given me, and discovered that one of those homes was his.

I parked in the circular driveway and rechecked the address, to make sure I was at the right residence.

"Right on schedule, Hamfist," Fish called from the

wide two-door entrance. "You made another TOT (Time On Target)."

"Nice place, Fish!"

"Aw, it's just my humble little abode," he grinned, "Come on in, and I'll show you around."

"First," he continued, "I want you to meet Rachel."

Fish's wife stood in the doorway.

"Tom's anxious to show off the Captain's House we built last year," she said, as she extended her hand. "I'm Rachel."

"Great to meet you, Rachel. I'm Hamfist. With a house like this, I don't blame him."

"Well," Tom smiled, "it's only 6000 square feet. But it's the view I'm really in love with."

I turned to follow his gaze, and marveled at the gorgeous vista.

"That's Pike's Peak over there," he said, pointing toward the south, "and Mount Evans over there, to the north. And we have the rest of the Front Range to greet us every time we open our door."

Pikes Peak had a sugary dusting of snow, standing in stark contrast to the clear, dark blue sky. The view was magnificent.

"Beautiful," I responded, "Now let me see how an airline pilot lives."

Tom guided me through his home, and I was more impressed with every room we entered. The main house was on one level, and there was a finished basement downstairs. The finished basement had a study, an exercise room and an additional bedroom with a private bath. On the main level, there was a huge kitchen with a stand-alone island complete with cook-top, a living room, a family room, and two bedroom suites, each with private bathrooms and walk-in closets.

"Wow!" I marveled, "You've come a long way since DaNang!"

"I've been really lucky," Fish answered. "Are you hungry? We're going to have fish, but this time, we're going to cook it before we eat it."

Apparently, he hadn't been as crazy about our sushi lunch as I was. But he'd been a good sport.

When we sat down, Fish brought out a bottle of fine wine and showed me the label. "How's this look for us tonight?"

"Sorry, Fish, I don't want to be rude, but I don't drink anymore."

Fish looked at me like I had two heads. "Are you sure you're the real Hamfist? Maybe I need to look under your bed for pods, to see if the body snatchers have replaced you."

"Long story, Fish, but I made a promise to my wife that I'd quit drinking. You remember how I would get when I was drunk. So I just quit."

"Wow. Not a problem, I'm just amazed that she got you to do it." He paused. "Good for her!"

Fish had seen me when I'd gotten drunk at DaNang, and had pulled me out of more than one bad situation when I'd blacked out. He'd never said anything about my drinking, but I could tell he was glad to see I'd quit.

Over dinner, Fish and Rachel took turns telling me how they'd met while he was in B-52 training. Rachel had been working at a travel agency in Atwater, the town just outside the base. Fish had gone in to buy some airline tickets, and they'd hit it off immediately. They'd gotten married just as Fish completed training, and he separated from the Air Force two months later and got snapped up by WorldJet almost immediately. It was exactly like he had said in his letter to Strategic Air Command when we were at DaNang – he had a Date of Separation, and it was ridiculous for the Air Force to spend money training him if he was about to leave the Air Force.

"Sounds like you guys have had a storybook life," I observed.

"We really have, Hamfist," Fish replied, "You know, if you ever decide to leave the Air Force…"

The sound of the doorbell interrupted our conversation. Fish got up from his seat.

"I invited someone over," he remarked as he approached the door, "He said he'd like to meet you."

A large man, probably in his late forties, was standing outside the door.

"Come on in, boss," Fish said, as they shook hands. Fish turned to me. "Hamfist, this is Todd Warner, our Vice President of Flight Operations."

"Pleased to meet you, sir," I said, as I shook his hand. He had a really firm grip.

"The pleasure is all mine, Captain Hancock. Or should I call you Hamfist?"

"Either name, sir."

We walked into the family room and sat around the coffee table.

"Hamfist, I can't begin to tell you how much we appreciate what you did on Flight 338 today. I don't know what would have happened if you hadn't been there. Our FOM has strict rules about both pilots not eating the same crew meal entrees during flight, but we hadn't addressed preflight eating. That's going to change."

"Excuse me, sir, what's an FOM?"

"Oh, sorry. It's the Flight Operations Manual, similar to your Air Force Regulation 60-1. It tells precisely what can and cannot be done. Like I said, we never considered what would happen if both pilots ate the same thing for breakfast at the same restaurant. Apparently the breakfast buffet at the Orlando airport had some problems. Lots of people who ate there got sick afterwords. Severe food poisoning."

I thought of how close I'd been to eating that same buffet.

"Do you train the Flight Attendants what to do if both pilots get sick, like today?"

"Not really." Todd looked a bit embarrassed. "We teach them to avoid passing liquids over the center pedestal, teach them a little about cockpit protocols, that's about it. The 737-200 doesn't have auto-land capabilities, so we can't even teach them how to operate the autopilot. Typically, on our higher-density routes, we have dead-heading pilots. Guys traveling to or from either work or training, especially on the Denver flights. Sometimes we have jump-seaters. Today was a rare exception."

"Well, I'm glad I was able to help."

"Listen, Hamfist," Todd said as he lowered his voice and leaned forward, "I'm telling you this strictly off the record. We have a formalized hiring process at WorldJet, a process that's been coordinated with the pilot union. There's a mini-physical, a simulator evaluation, some psychological testing, the Stanine Test, and an interview." He leaned further forward. "But, just between us girls," he smiled, "that will just be a formality for you. If you want to be an airline pilot, there's a job waiting for you at WorldJet. The way we're expanding right now, I would expect you'll make Captain in four years."

I didn't really know how to react. I was surprised and flattered. And, although I hadn't been actively trying to get an airline job, seeing Fish's lifestyle really made an impression on me. Great pay and eighteen days a month off would really give me the opportunity to do things with, and for, my family that I hadn't been able to do in the Air Force. And I had been getting more disillusioned with the Air Force with every passing day. Maybe, I thought, I should consider the airlines.

"I'm really honored, sir, and flattered. I hadn't given a lot of thought to airline flying, but, I have to say, it was pretty cool flying that big jet."

"I can't give you an answer right now," I continued, "I need to discuss this with my family before I make a decision."

"I understand completely," he responded, reaching into his shirt pocket. "Here's my business card, and this," he pulled a pen out of his shirt pocket and wrote on the card, "is my personal phone number. Give me a call when you're ready to leave the Air Force."

"Thank you, sir. I will."

70

March 17, 1978

My first night in Denver, I had called Sam and told her about flying the Guppy and meeting up with Fish again. And I had related to her about the incredible number of days off the WorldJet pilots got in their monthly schedules. It was intriguing. Very intriguing.

Now it was time for us to have a serious discussion about our future plans. Sam was aware, naturally, that I had become disillusioned with the Air Force. At every assignment, I would hear about the "Real Air Force", some mythical construct that didn't exist at whatever base I was currently stationed at, but was promised to magically appear when I would get to my next assignment. The Real Air Force was like the pot of gold at the end of a rainbow, always almost within reach, never quite attainable.

It hadn't been all bad. I'll admit, I had enjoyed Undergraduate Pilot Training. There was the typical level of bullshit, of course, but I had become used to a much higher level of abuse during my four years at the Academy. And I had really enjoyed flying the O-2 in combat in Vietnam. Although I wasn't in a fighter, it was a damn rewarding mission, with much more responsibility than a normal Lieutenant would experience. But the O-2 assignment itself represented a bit of sleight-of-hand that the Air Force, unfortunately, was very good at. The promise had been that the Distinguished Graduate of any UPT class would get his choice of aircraft following graduation, but the nebulous "needs of the service" had put me in the smallest, slowest airplane in the inventory.

Then the promise of "volunteer for Vietnam and you'll get your choice of aircraft when you return from combat" turned, again, to vapor. I had received a B-52 assignment, and if General McCall hadn't interceded, that's what I would have gotten.

I, and I alone, was responsible for getting the T-39 assignment to Yokota, but I hadn't anticipated the extensive TDY that would entail. And when I volunteered for a second Vietnam tour, in the F-4, I got it, so I wasn't getting screwed at every turn.

And flying the F-4 in combat was a dream come true. Yeah, there was the typical bullshit of ridiculous targets being fragged, like some of the insignificant nitnoy bridges in Hanoi. But, overall, it was great flying. Every mission was like a John Wayne movie. And I had an exceptionally rewarding tour.

But then, the peacetime Air Force, even flying F-4s, was really a drag. Like Colonel Wilson had said, fighter pilots in the peacetime Air force are puppets on a string.

And like the old saying went, if the Air Force had wanted pilots to have families, they would have issued them.

The biggest disappointment was the quality of leadership I was seeing. Actually, it was lack of leadership. The people I had been working for, after Vietnam, were nothing like the exceptional examples of great leaders I had seen on a daily basis at the Academy. As far as leadership was concerned, most of the people I had worked for were really mediocre.

And then there was the Air Force Song. My entire life, ever since I was a kid, I would get goose bumps whenever I heard "Off we go, into the wild blue yonder". I had learned the lyrics at a young age, and had actually gotten into a lot of trouble at the Academy, as a doolie, when I had been commanded to recite them at the dinner table. I had ended the song, "Nothing can stop the Army Air Corps", which was the way I had learned it as a child. After the Air Force became a separate service, the words had been changed to "Nothing can stop the U.S. Air Force". I did my share of push-ups for that misquote!

But now, hearing the song did nothing for me. In fact, I would feel a sense of melancholy with the realization that the chill was gone. Now it was just another song.

I'd been in the Air Force for eleven years, actually

fifteen if you count the time at the Academy, and I was still waiting to see the Real Air Force, the one with great leadership. And if I stayed in for nine more years, to get to retirement, what then? I'd be much older, maybe too old to go to the airlines or start a different career. In a way, I felt like being in the Air Force was like sitting in a warm bath in a cold room. Sooner or later, the bath, and the room, would get colder, and I'd have to get out. Maybe it was time to do it now.

And I was starting to see a level of downright nastiness in the Air Force that I had never before experienced. A great example is the way they unilaterally extended everyone's Active Duty Service Commitment.

Every pilot would pick up a commitment, usually two years or more, for attending any kind of advanced training. Whenever a pilot received an assignment that required him to attend an RTU, with a training commitment, he had the option to either accept the assignment or leave the Air Force, if his original commitment was already completed. If he still had time remaining on his previous commitment, he could "put in his papers" – request a Date of Separation at the end of his current commitment – and not be saddled with any additional commitment. He may or may not still receive the assignment and the training, but he would not receive any additional commitment.

That was what Beans Beaner had done. He had a

year remaining on his original Active Duty Service Commitment from F-4 RTU, so when he got his O-2 assignment, he put in his papers. He still went to O-2 training, but didn't incur any additional commitment. A year later, he separated from the Air Force.

So, whenever a pilot had an assignment that required training, he would be informed of the commitment the training would trigger. Each jock went into it with his eyes open.

When I went through O-2 training at Patrick, I picked up a two-year commitment, the same as someone who had never flown the aircraft before. That was okay with me – I was a "lifer" anyway. That was then.

One of the guys in my squadron, Bill Blue, was scheduled to go to the Personnel Office for an annual Records Review. The Records Review afforded an officer the opportunity to see what was in his official records, and dispute any erroneous information. Typically, the pilot would get to see all of his previous OERs, his training records, his record of PME, and the dates of his Active Duty Service Commitment. When Bill saw his commitment date, he was flabbergasted. The commitment for his attendance at O-2 training was shown as four years!

"I was told the commitment for O-2 training was two years. I have it in writing," he protested.

"Yes sir," the Sergeant at Personnel replied, "it was two years when you attended training, but about six months ago they changed the commitment for O-2 RTU to four years."

"But I attended two years ago!"

"Yes, sir, but Headquarters Air Force adjusted everyone's commitment date to reflect the new commitment."

Bill stormed out of the Personnel Office and called his father. His father was a Congressman.

As soon as we heard about what happened to Bill, all of us in the squadron made appointments for Records Reviews, and all of us discovered that our commitments had been extended without our knowledge. Every one of us, including me.

Obviously, that was illegal as hell. When I told Sam about it, she was livid.

"That's an ex-post-facto decree," she said, becoming an attorney again, "It sounds like the Air Force is trying to make everyone indentured servants."

Those of us who had been leaning toward getting out of the Air Force had just received a giant push. Those of us on the fence, lifers like me, got edged toward leaving.

Bill's dad raised a huge stink about the nefarious

actions of someone, somewhere in the Personnel food chain, and ultimately we all had our commitment dates re-adjusted back to the original dates. But we had all been placed on notice that the Air Force could fuck with us at any time. Our collective trust had been destroyed. Seventeen guys in my squadron who had been undecided about separating from the Air Force put in their papers during the next month.

I was one of them.

71

March 17, 1978

Sam looked into my eyes as we sat opposite each other at the kitchen table.

"Ham," she said, as she reached across the table to hold my hand, "whatever decision you make is fine with me. I love you and I want to support you in whatever you decide to do."

"When we first went out," she continued, "when we were in Rappongi at the Hamburger Inn, talking, you had mentioned you some day wanted to be an airline pilot. But first you wanted to be a fighter pilot. Well, you got to be a fighter pilot. Now I think it's time to pursue your other dream."

"You don't think I'm being selfish, do you?"

"It's not selfish to do something you want to do, as long as it doesn't hurt anyone else. Johnnie, Tommy and I will be fine. You'll be gone a lot more than you are now, but you'll have more time off. You'll be able to spend more time with us when you're home. And after the first year you'll be making the same amount as you're getting in the Air Force right now. And we'll get to travel, a lot, for free. I'm getting excited just thinking about it."

"You're sure?" I asked, "If you want, I can pull my papers and stay in."

"What would you do if you didn't have Johnny, Tommy and me to worry about?"

"I'd get out and fly for WorldJet."

"Then, that's what I want you to do. Remember how you told me that once a pilot makes a decision, he should stick to it?"

Long ago I had explained to Sam about the decision-making process during flight. If a pilot can't see the runway at the minimum altitude on an instrument approach and decides to go-around, he should stick with his decision, even if he later sees the runway as he's climbing out.

"Yes."

"Okay, then," she said, "the decision is made. Let's get started on the rest of our lives."

Johnny giggled as I gave Sam a long, passionate kiss.

"Okay," I said, "I need to make a phone call."

I went to my desk, retrieved Todd Warner's

business card, and dialed his personal number.

The adventure continues . . .

Follow the adventures of Hamfist Hancock here at:

http://www.genolly.com

http://www.hamfistAdventures.com

Stay in touch with the author via:

Twitter: http://twitter.com/gnolly

If you liked *Hamfist Out*, please post a review.

Other books by G.E.Nolly:

Hamfist Over The Trail

Hamfist Down!

Hamfist Over Hanoi

ABOUT THE AUTHOR

George Nolly served as a pilot in the United States Air Force, flying 315 combat missions on two successive tours of duty in Vietnam, earning 3 Distinguished Flying Crosses and 24 Air Medals flying O-2A and F-4 aircraft. In 1983, George received Tactical Air Command Instructor of the Year Award for his service as an instructor in the Air Force Forward Air Controller Course. Following his Air Force duty, he hired on with United Airlines and rose to the position of B-777 Check Captain, and also served as a Federal Flight Deck Officer. Following his retirement from United, George accepted a position as a B-777 Captain with Jet airways, operating throughout Europe, Asia and the Middle East. In 2000, George was selected as a Champion in the Body-for-LIFE Transformation Challenge, and is a Certified Fitness Trainer and self-defense expert with more than 30 years' experience in combative arts. George received a Bachelor of Science Degree from the United States Air Force Academy and a Master of Science Degree, in Systems Management, from the University of Southern California. He completed all of the required studies for a second Master of Science Degree, in Education, and received his Doctor of Business Administration Degree, specializing in Homeland Security, from Northcentral University. He now flight instructs in the B777 and B787.

GLOSSARY OF TERMS

AO – Area of Operations

BDA – Bomb Damage Assessment

Below the zone – Promotion earlier than normal sequence

BOQ – Bachelor Officer's Quarters

CBU – Cluster Bomb Unit

DEROS – Date Eligible for Return from OverSeas

DOS – Date of Separation

ETA – Estimated Time of Arrival

FAC – Forward Air Controller

Fingertip – Close formation flying, 3-foot wingtip spacing

Gomer – Guy On Motorable Enemy Route

Initial – The first portion of a visual overhead landing pattern

IP – Instructor Pilot

M-1 maneuver – grunting to increase thoracic pressure

Mark 82 – A 500-pound bomb

MiG – Russian fighter jet, Mikoyan and Gurevich

Mike-mike - millimeter

MPC – Military Personnel Center

Nape - Napalm

OER – Officer Effectiveness Report

PCS – Permanent Change of Station

PDA – Public Display of Affection

Piddle pack – Portable urinal

RNO – Results Not Observed

SAM – Surface to Air Missile

Short-timer – Someone nearing DEROS

Slicks – Bombs with no high-drag metal parachute fins

Snake – Bombs with metal parachute fins

TDY – Temporary Duty

TOT – Time Over Target

URC-64 – Portable Survival Radio

VOQ – Visiting Officer's Quarters

Willie Pete – White phosphorous rocket